LOVE IN THE AIR

MARIAH ANKENMAN

CONTENTS

EDITED by Angela James

DEDICATION

To my aerial family at Gravity.

CONTENT WARNING

Love in the Air is a fun, open door steamy romance with a happy ending, but there are a few on page discussions that may be triggering for some readers. Discussions of alcoholic parents, cancer, death of a sibling. Please read with care.

1
_____

Hate was a very strong word. One Izadora Grant tried her best not to use, especially not for people. However, the man standing in front of her with his cocky, shit-eating grin warranted use of the word multiple times over.

"You've got to be fucking kidding me!"

His smile grew wider. "Hey, Iz. Long time."

Not long enough by her count. It had been eight years since her high school graduation. Eight years since the day she looked her nemesis in the eye and wished him goodbye with as much pleasantry as she could muster (she might dislike the guy, but she wasn't a complete monster). Eight years since she breathed a sigh of relief knowing she'd never have to deal with Chance O'Brien ever again.

And yet here he was, standing five feet away, grinning at her like the time he beat her in the school science fair.

Fucking A!

"Chance," she muttered through clenched teeth. "What the hel—I mean, what are you doing here?"

He turned his head, taking in the large room around

them filled with tumbling mats, silks and hoops hanging from the twenty-foot ceilings, and people in tightly fitted yoga clothes milling about.

"Same thing as you, I imagine."

Oh no! Oh, please don't let the next words out of his mouth be—

"I'm with the company."

Dammit!

Iz sucked in a deep, calming breath. Or she tried to anyway. The furious pounding in her chest reminded her she was far from anything resembling calm. Calm had always been a hard reach around Chance. She couldn't help it; the guy pressed every single one of her buttons. In school, they'd always been competing. For grades, parts in the school plays, scholarships, even homecoming dates.

One would think since they were both were members of their high school's LGBTQ+ Alliance, they would be friends. After all, as a Pansexual woman she was used to having people dismiss her sexuality as not real or simply waiting to "pick a side" and she knew Chance as a Bisexual man got the same treatment. But just because they were on the same team, didn't mean she had to like the guy. Especially since Kelly Fritz picked Chance over Iz for senior prom.

That heartbreak still stung.

Trying her best not to let their past color her present, Iz forced a smile. "I didn't realize you were still into aerials."

They'd both been on the high school gymnastic team, which had a minor component of aerial training. Iz had fallen in love with the lyra and continued her hoop study during college and beyond. It had always been her dream to join a company and travel the world. Now she'd finally achieved her goal. But it looked like fate was giving her a big middle finger if the man in front of her had crashed her dream.

"Yeah." His smile grew, white teeth blinding against the dark hairs of his closely trimmed beard. "I tried out trapeze, rope, and straps—and not just the aerial kind."

She ignored his wink. Chance always loved to get a rise out of her by saying outrageous things. It seemed the man hadn't matured past high school. She scoffed, big surprise.

"But hoop will always be my first love."

On that, they could agree. And *only* that.

"You look great, Iz. How's life?"

Seriously? Were they really doing this? Just because it appeared they were working in the same company didn't mean they had to get all chummy. Did he conveniently forget how much they annoyed each other? Scratch that, he annoyed her. She, however, seemed to have little effect on him.

"It's fine."

A deep rumble of laughter escaped him. "Loquacious as ever, I see."

She held back a growl. Dick. He was baiting her on purpose. Well, two could play at that game.

"Wow, big word, Chance. You must have brushed up on your vocabulary since I trounced your ass in the sophomore spelling bee."

His smile tightened for a moment before he shook his head with a chuckle. "Same old Iz. Guess I'll see ya around."

With that, he turned and headed off toward a small group who were stretching. She watched with narrow eyes as Chance sat and started easily conversing with the group. She knew a few of the people he sat with. Some were from the studio she trained at. And now they were all here.

Sky Dancers company had held open auditions last

month. Aerialists from the Denver metro area and even as far as Colorado Springs and Boulder came and auditioned. There were students from every aerial school along the front range here.

But why did he have to get in?

"Why do you look like someone ran over your cat?"

Iz jumped at the voice behind her. Turning, she came face to face with her best friend. A calm sense of relief filled her chest. At least her bestie got cast in the company too. She could survive a year of touring with Chance as long as Tori was by her side.

"I don't have a cat," she responded.

Tori shrugged. "Fine, then what's with the death scowl?"

She didn't have a death scowl.

A quick focus of her body let Iz know she was full of it. Every muscle was tight, including her jaw, and she felt the pull of her eyebrows. Crap, this wasn't the energy she needed right now. Focusing her intentions, she unclenched her muscles, relaxing her body and face into a neutral position. She needed to make friends, be open and warm.

Fitting in wasn't always easy for her, but she'd been working on being more open and friendly. These people would basically be her family for the next year. She had to get along with them.

Her gaze slipped back to Chance, laughing at something Derek from her studio said.

Okay, maybe she didn't have to get along with everybody.

"Why are you glaring at tall, hairy, and handsome?"

"He's not handsome, he's an ass," she answered her bestie.

"Babe, you know I love you and your quirky sense of taste, but that guy is hot with a capital H."

Shit. Tori was right. Chance had always been good looking, even in high school. Which was probably how he got so
many more dates than her. But the years had been even
kinder to him. The fitted joggers and tight tank top he wore
revealed he'd kept up with his training, like he said. His
clothing couldn't hide the well-defined muscles his body
had honed.

He'd covered the jaw line everyone obsessed over in
school with a close-cropped beard that somehow made the
angle of his face even more delicious, and he'd tied his dark
brown hair into a bun on the top of his head. For a moment,
she wondered how long it was when he undid it. Shaking
her head with a scowl, she chastised herself for the wayward
thought. She didn't care about how long his hair was, or
anything else about the man.

Fine, he was hot. Didn't change the fact that she hated
him and always would.

"Chance is an ass."

Tori's brow went up. "You know him?"

"Knew him," she corrected. "We went to high school
together."

Her friend's mouth dropped open. "Wait, is that the guy
who tormented you?"

"Shhhh." She waved a hand at her friend, pulling her to
the side when a few heads swung in their direction. "Keep
your voice down."

Tori winced. "Sorry."

Her friend had volume filter issues, but Iz didn't mind,
especially considering Tori put up with a host of issues she
had. It was why they were besties.

"Tormented is a strong word," she said in a hushed
voice.

"Not from the stories you told me." Tori glared at

Chance. "He took your scholarship, stole your prom date, and ruined your favorite sweater."

She winced. Okay, maybe in her sharing she'd...embellished a little.

"Technically, he beat me out for the scholarship. Kelly picked him over me for prom, and the sweater thing was an accident."

He'd tripped over her backpack and spilled an entire can of paint over her in scene shop class. To his credit, Chance had apologized profusely, but teenage Iz had seen it as yet another attack from her nemesis and chewed him out for it, resulting in both of them being sent to the office.

"I can't believe he got into the company, too." She moved so her back was to Chance and started warming up. "I'd kind of hoped he moved to Australia or some other island far away with no way to get to it but a boat or plane."

She certainly never imagined running into him again like this.

"You gonna be okay?" Tori asked as she moved to Iz's side and joined her in downward dog.

Iz peddled her feet, stretching her calves. "Yeah. It's a big company. What are the chances we'll have to work closely together?"

Hopefully slim to none.

The Sky Dancers company had fifty performers who would cycle in and out of the fifteen act show the directors had created. It was a beautiful vision filled with all the aerial apparatuses and a yearlong contract that included international travel and performance. Something Iz had wanted her entire life. And she would not let the fact that her old nemesis was in the cast ruin this opportunity for her. She could be a mature adult.

"I can play nice."

Tori barked out a laugh, quickly smothering it when Iz glared at her underneath her armpit.

"Sorry, babe, but you suck at playing nice." Tori moved forward into cobra position.

Dammit, she was right. Iz sucked at pretending to like someone or something when she didn't. Hell, she had issues showing positive emotions when she did like someone. A complaint from many a previous partner. The breakup line "you're too walled up, I never know what you're feeling" had been uttered by more than one person during her breakups. Some people might find that odd, but she found it to be the truth.

Iz didn't do lovey-dovey stuff well. All the emotional vulnerability? No thank you. She never understood how people could let themselves be exposed like that. How did you trust someone with your heart when they could so easily rip it from your chest and stomp on it?

Like her dad did to her mom when he left.

Whatever. She didn't need a relationship when she had a box of toys all curated to her pleasure at home. Besides, she had a show to focus on now.

"Okay everybody," Jen, the co-owner of Sky Dancers, called out. "Gather up!"

There was a mass shuffling as everyone in the room paused in their warm-ups to gather in a large circle around Jen and Meg, the two owners of the company. Iz sighed as she found herself directly across from Chance. No way of keeping him out of sight now. She forced a tight smile as he caught her eye and winked. Smug bastard. Turning her attention to her new bosses, she tuned him out and focused on what Jen was saying.

"We want to welcome you all to the Sky Dancers family. Auditions were tough, but you've all proved you deserve a spot in this company, and we can't wait to take this show on the road."

A loud, roaring cheer rose from the crowd surrounding her. Excitement coursed through her body, nerves dancing along her spine as the thrill of what she was about to embark on truly hit her. Glee had her feet bouncing in place as the crowd quieted down.

"Now," Meg said, picking up where Jen left off. "We only have five weeks of rehearsal before we head to our first show in New York, and then we're off for the European leg of the schedule."

Yes! It was a dream come true. Iz had never been outside the United States before and to go doing something she loved...she had to pinch herself to remember it was real and not some wild fantasy come to life.

Jen moved to the far wall, where she tacked up a piece of paper while Meg explained.

"Jen is posting the show acts. We've carefully selected each performer for their specific acts based on your auditions. As you know, the show's theme is Connections in the Ether, so we've grouped and paired you up to perform pieces reflecting the theme."

Her bouncing intensified. Iz wanted to run to the wall and see what she got, who she was grouped with. She hoped she'd get to perform a piece with Tori, but since her friend did mostly silk and she specialized in lyra, she doubted it. Didn't matter in the long run, whoever she ended up with she knew it was going to be amazing.

"Your partners and rehearsal times are listed on the sheet, along with companywide rehearsal times. Again, we're so excited to have you all join the Sky Dancers family. Now let's do this!"

There was another roaring cheer and a mad rush to the

wall as everyone scrambled to see what they would be performing. Knowing her friend didn't like crowds, Iz hung back with Tori until there was a bit of a gap.

"Iz!" Tori exclaimed, jumping up and down and she turned from the sheet. "We get to do a group act together!"

She stepped forward to see the sheet, scanning the list to see that in fact there was a group act of silks and lyra and the group of performers included her and her bestie. Her smile grew as she noticed another act she was in, all hoop this time. But as her gaze scanned down the list, the warm feelings died. She blinked as she read her name paired with another in a duo act. Not only a duo act, but a single hoop duo act.

Normally, that'd be fine. She'd done plenty of two person acts before on a single hoop. She loved them. There was a beauty in two people twining around one hoop. The act itself didn't bother her. It was the name next to her own that sent a cold sliver of dread through her.

"Well, look at that, Iz." Chance's chuckles sounded dangerously close to her ear. "Looks like you and me got the lover's duet piece."

Fuck.

2

If looks could kill, Chance would be a dead man.

Iz's light brown eyes narrowed. He imagined laser beams coming out of her eyes, boring into him, like a character in those manga books she used to carry around with her everywhere back in school. It still blew his mind that he was standing in front of her after all this time. He'd figured Iz would have moved as far away as possible after they graduated high school. It was what she always claimed she'd do. She'd always talked about how she was going to travel, see the world.

She's going to do that now. We both are.

His chest warmed at the reminder. The opportunity that lay before him. The promise he would get to keep to his brother.

"Un-fucking-believable!" she swore under her breath.

He laughed, couldn't help it. Riling Iz up had always been a good time. He loved the fiery challenge she got in her eyes whenever he pushed her buttons. Immature? Maybe, but old habits died hard.

"Aw, now come on, Iz. Don't be like that or I might get the impression you don't like me."

He didn't think it was possible, but her eyes narrowed even further until all he could see was the tiniest peek of her iris behind long, dark lashes. Still the same feisty Iz. She hadn't grown even an inch since he last saw her. He still towered over her tiny five-foot frame, but the intricate works of inked art all along her arms were new. So was the light peach hair color she was sporting.

Such an odd choice. The soft, warm color was in direct contrast to the sharpness of her attitude. Or maybe it was just him who brought the fight out of Iz. As much as she put up a front of badass ice queen, he knew better. He knew in school she volunteered to help tutor anyone in their math class who needed it. Iz always headed up the donation drive for their town's local food bank. And she'd helped Susan, their school's nighttime maintenance manager clean the school for an entire week after the woman had minor surgery. Yeah, Iz was a big 'ol softie.

To everyone, but him.

"Cut the crap, Chance. Let's not pretend we ever liked each other."

There's where she was wrong. Not that he'd ever say that to her—telling Izadora Grant she was wrong was a death wish for sure—but he did like her. Always had. The tiny fireball of smarts and sass had challenged him every day in high school. He was fairly certain that if it hadn't been for Iz competing with him, he never would have pushed himself so hard and beaten her out for that scholarship. He appreciated Iz's competitive spirit, and he genuinely liked her. When she wasn't verbally castrating him.

Okay, maybe a tiny, unbalanced part of him liked it when she did that too.

Iz glanced around the room, desperation etched on her face. "Maybe we can switch partners."

"Would it really be that bad to perform with me?"

Her gaze whipped back to him, brow arched. Ouch. He knew she didn't care for him, but did she have to make her disgust so plainly obvious?

"Look." He moved closer, lowering his voice. "I don't think it's the best idea for us to start off this show causing waves. It's only one act and—"

"Izadora! Chance!" Jen's cheerful voice sounded from behind him. "Meg and I loved both of your auditions and we think your piece together is going to be phenomenal. Have you two gotten a chance to introduce yourselves?"

Turning, Chance smiled at the company co-owner. "Hey, Jen, actually me and Iz go way back."

"You do?" The tall woman blinked, a smile replacing her shock. "Wonderful! Oh, this is great. A piece like this is always better when the performers have a personal connection."

Yeah, he wasn't so sure about that. Hard to perform a believable lover's duet when your partner would rather kill you than kiss you.

"Group conditioning starts in fifteen," Jen said, waving as she turned and headed over to talk to another group gathered a few feet away.

"Why did you say that?" Iz hissed in a hushed voice.

He searched his earlier words, wondering what she was pissed about now.

"Um, because we do go way back."

"You made it sound like we're old friends."

For the life of him, he couldn't understand why she was so upset. Why was it a bad thing if the owner of the company thought they were friends?

"Failing to see the problem."

A heavy sigh left her as her eyes rolled upwards. Oh goody, he knew what was coming next. A classic Iz talking down. Where Iz got on her high horse and talked to him like he was the biggest moron out there. While he loved trading barbs with her, he really didn't appreciate when she insinuated he was stupid. He was the one who scored higher than her on the ACT's.

"Look, Iz." He held up a hand as she opened her mouth. "As much as it sucks, we've been paired together for this act. This *one* act. I know as well as you that there are a dozen other aerialist who didn't get into this show who would love the opportunity to take our spots."

That got her mouth closed. A tiny frown marred her brow. She waved for him to continue.

"If we cause too much of a fuss, they'll kick us out and replace us."

Aerialist might not be the highest demand in the performer world, but he knew a performer could be replaced for any reason, and he wasn't risking this opportunity.

"I can't lose this gig." He'd already lost too much, losing this wasn't an option.

"Me either," she agreed. "So, what do we do?"

He figured it was obvious, but if she needed it spelled out, "We fake it."

"Fake it?"

He glanced around, making sure everyone was still occupied with their own shit, not paying attention to them. Lowering his voice, he leaned in closer, so close he could smell the hint of flowers wafting up from Iz's hair. So sweet and inviting. The juxtaposition made his lips curl in a smile.

"We need to pretend to get along."

"Fake a friendship?" she asked, as if he just suggested they run off to Vegas and get married.

"Better than getting kicked out of the show for ripping each other's heads off."

She scoffed. "Oh, come on now, Chance. You know I'd never do something as violent as rip your head off. Far too messy." Her lips curled in a devious grin. "I'd poison you. Clean, efficient, and with the right ingredients, untraceable."

He leaned back, a hint of uncertainty swirling in his gut. He was ninety percent sure she was kidding. A gleeful glint lit her eyes. Seventy-five percent sure.

"Remind me never to accept cookies from you."

She snorted. "As if I'd ever make you cookies."

"Only the kind with poison in them."

'Okay." She sighed. "You might have a point."

What now? He blinked at her one-eighty. "Did you just admit I'm right?"

"Never." She scowled, but there was a hint of a smile curling her lips.

He held in his laughed. They were making headway. He didn't want to screw it up. And Laughing at Iz was a sure way to get a knee to the nuts. He preferred his testicles where they were, and unharmed, thank you very much.

"But," she continued. "We need to get along to perform together and now that you told Jen we're friends, it's not like I can request a new partner."

Technically, he said they knew each other, Jen simply inferred it meant they were friends, and he didn't correct her. But having their bosses think they were friends was a good thing. You wanted to get along with the people you'd be traveling the world with for the next year.

He had no illusions that this entire experience would be sunshine and rainbows. They were all artists after all, and artists were...well, temperamental. But he and Iz needed to bury the hatchet—or at least appear to get along—if they wanted to survive this thing without getting fired. He could do it if she could.

"Fake friends?" he asked, holding out his hand.

Iz stared at his palm like it was a snake that might jump up and bite her. His gut clenched as he waited, hand outstretched. He needed her in this with him. He was not getting fired. This was his chance to fulfill his promise to his brother. His chance to finally make up for his failings. He would go on this tour and he wouldn't let something like Iz's lifelong hate for him ruin it.

The breath he was holding eased out of his chest when she sighed and placed her palm in his.

"Fine, fake friends. At the studio only," she added, glaring at him. "I'm not gonna be all buddy-buddy with you outside of rehearsals and performances. This is strictly for show."

"Deal." He shook her hand, feeling the same rough calluses he knew covered his own from hours of practice. A small spark of awareness traveled up his arm at the contact. He frowned, pulling his hand away quickly.

What the hell was that?

Static. Had to be something like that. With all the silks rigged in here, there was bound to be some charge in the air. At least Iz hadn't seemed to notice anything, judging by the determined expression on her face.

"Great, all we have to do is pretend to get along in front of everyone and everything will be fine," she said with a nod.

Not exactly. They also had to spend hours together practicing and performing. They had to learn to trust each other not to fuck up their routine. A fuck up in aerials could result in broken bones, or worse. And they would have to spend a lot of time in close contact, their bodies intertwined around the hoop. Depending on the routine Jen and Meg set for them, he and Iz were about to get real up close and personal with the physical contact.

Shit!

Maybe he hadn't thought this through entirely.

Too late to turn back now. They were doing this. Sink or swim, this fake friendship was a go and if he wanted to keep his promise to his brother, he needed to focus on playing nice with Iz for a change.

"Time for conditioning, everyone," Meg called out from the center of the room. "Grab an apparatus and let's start with straddle ups."

Iz smiled at him, a challenge lighting her eyes. "Bet I can do more than you."

Without waiting for his answer, she ran to a hoop on the far side of the room and started calling out her count as she gripped the hoop, straddling her legs and lifting them into the air as she inverted underneath the hoop, toes pointed to perfection. A small chuckle escaped his lips. The hammer had been thrown. He supposed friends could engage in a healthy dose of competition.

"I'm ahead by three, O'Brien," she called to him as he took the hoop across from her. "Better hurry or you'll never catch up."

"Just giving you the head start you need, Grant."

Her eyes narrowed as she stared at him from her upside-down position, peach hair dangling beneath her.

"In your dreams, *buddy*."

He snorted as he started his set. Oh yeah, this plan of theirs was starting off with a bang. He wondered how long until it blew up in their faces.

3

"Please tell me that delicious smell coming from your bag is your famous chocolate protein bites."

Iz smiled at Tori as her friend arched her neck, trying to peek into Iz's tote. "It is."

Reaching deep into her bag past her back warmer, extra leggings, water bottle, and a host of other items necessary for rehearsal, Iz grabbed the plastic container filled with the tasty treat she'd made this afternoon.

"Gimme!" Tori reached for the bin.

Iz lifted it, which was ridiculous because her friend towered over her. Everyone towered over her. Still. "No grabby hands. I made these for everyone. I even used the gluten-free ingredients in case anyone has celiac."

"Trying to make a good impression?" Tori asked with a smile.

Of course she was. These people would basically be her family for the next year. They'd be traveling together, stuck for long periods of time with each other. Some of them she already knew from past shows and studios, but it never hurt to sweeten the pot. Besides, she enjoyed making food for people. The joy in their eyes when the flavors exploded on their tongue, the moans of delight as they bit into whatever treat she made. She loved that she could make people happy with her baked goods.

If she hadn't gone into graphic design, Iz might have even tried her hand at becoming a baker. Unfortunately, the hours required to be a baker never would have worked. The beauty of her current job was she could do it freelance, on her own time and, with the internet, she could work from anywhere. Which meant she could still get some work in on this tour. A good thing, since the show didn't exactly pay handsomely. At least all the travel and lodging cost were covered.

"Full stomachs make friends," she repeated her mother's oft saying. "It's how we became friends."

Tori snorted. "No, we went on a terrible first date and decided we would be a horrible couple, but the very best of buddies."

Oh, right.

"I still say I won you over to the friendship side with my strawberry tarts."

"Oh God." Tori moaned. "Those things are so good. When are you making them for me again?"

"Your birthday." It was tradition.

Tori groaned. "But that's five months away!"

"Anticipation makes them taste better."

"No, I'm pretty sure it's the brandy you add."

Iz nodded. "True. Now let's pass these out and make more friends."

There was a fair number of performers already in the studio, but a few people were still arriving. Iz moved around the groups, passing out the treat she made, relaying all the ingredients, and keeping a mental note of anyone who said they had an allergy. She loved bringing in tasty treats for people, but she would feel awful if she accidently poisoned someone.

"Looks like someone else is making the friendship rounds," Tori said, nodding to the far end of the room.

Glancing over, Iz saw Chance standing with a group of people, all smiles and laughter. Her bright mood soured. Okay, maybe she wouldn't feel bad about poisoning one person. Not badly, just a little tummy trouble to wipe the know-it-all grin off his face for an hour or two.

"I heard he's from the AirCirque studio. The one in Boulder."

Iz nodded. That explained why they'd never crossed paths in the aerial world then. Boulder wasn't too far from Denver, but she never ventured up that way for studios. She stuck to the city.

"You gonna be okay to perform with him?"

Her friend's eyes held a hint of concern. Iz smiled, giving Tori a quick side hug.

"I'll be fine. We came to an understanding."

"Really?" Tori arched a brow. "An understanding?"

She shrugged. "Yeah, for the sake of the show, Chance and I will be friendly and polite to each other."

Tori barked out a laugh, smothering it with her hand at Iz's dark look.

"What?"

"I'm sorry, babe, you know I love you, but faking your true feelings...isn't really your strong suit."

Hey! She could fake it with the best of them.

"Hey, Iz," a deep, annoyingly familiar voice said. "Who's your friend?"

She took a deep breath and unclenched her jaw. Now was the perfect time to prove how good at faking it she was.

To Tori, Chance, and everyone. Pasting a bright smile on her face, she turned and stared Chance directly in the eyes.

"Oh hey, Chance. It's so good to see you. I can't wait to start working on our routine. This is my best friend, Tori. Tori, this is my buddy Chance from high school. He's such a great guy."

Chance stared at her as if she'd grown a second head. The air around them stilled as no one spoke. Quiet muffles of conversations around them filled the silence. Her jaw ached from the forced smile, but she refused to let it drop.

Finally, Chance leaned in close and whispered. "Are you okay? Blink once if that thing in your hand is a bomb and someone forced to bring it in here for a robbery. Did aliens abduct you? What am I saying? If they did, I'd be talking to alien Iz, not real Iz. Maybe you've been possessed by a demon who's trying to emulate human emotions?"

Her smile fell, annoyance bubbling to the surface.

"Okay, first, these are chocolate protein bites," she said, ripping the cover off the bin and shoving the half empty container toward him. "Who the hell would try to rob an aerial studio, and why? Second, I'm not an alien or possessed. I was trying to go for friendly."

He winced. "Next time tone down the Joker smile and try to take the murder out of your eyes."

She was two seconds away from shoving the entire bin of treats down his smartass throat.

"You do get murder eyes when you try to lie, Iz," Tori agreed.

"Hey!" Betrayed by her own bestie. This was not a good start to today's rehearsal.

"Chance," he said, holding his hand out to Tori. "*Buddy* from high school, I guess."

To her credit, Tori stared at Chance's hand for a moment before shaking it. A hint of warning on her bestie's face.

"Tori. I am her actual best friend and I've heard *all* about you, Chance O'Brien."

He cleared his throat, gaze moving back and forth between her and Tori. She couldn't help the smug smile that curled her lips. Her bestie was awesome.

"Oh, right. All of it bad, I assume?"

Tori shrugged.

"Okay then, well, in my defense, Iz is a badass at pretty much everything, except lying. I simply try to keep up. What's a little healthy dose of competition between friends, right Iz?"

"We're not friends." And she would not soften because he called her a badass. She was a badass. Chance was simply stating facts. So what if his praise made something inside her sit up and cheer? He would not sway her.

He leaned in, giving her pointed look and speaking in a hushed voice, "While we're in this building and on tour we are."

Damn, he had a point. The whole "dream job" on the line thing. With a sigh, she tried for a friendly smile again, a smaller, more believable one this time.

"Right, friends." Frenemies more like it.

Tori let out a small bark of laughter. "You two are going to have to work a lot harder than that if you want to convince everyone here you're best buddies."

They didn't have to be best buddies. They just had to pull off friendly. They could do that.

"Okay everybody," Jen called out from the center of the room. "Grab a partner and start stretching."

"Shall we work on it?" Chance asked, hand outstretched, indicating to the mats in front of them.

Her breath caught in her throat. She glanced to Tori, who she'd planned on warming up with, but her bestie waved a hand in the air and grabbed the bin from Iz's hands.

"I'll go warm up with Callie. You two work on playing nice."

Iz snorted. Playing nice with Chance. There was a situation she'd never imagined herself having to be in.

Swallowing down her protest, she followed him over to the blue and white colored mats lining the room. She sat next to him as they both straddled, stretching their legs.

"Pull stretches," Meg called out as she and Jen walked up and down the middle of the room, watching everyone stretch and offering help when needed.

Chance turned toward her. Iz scooted until she faced him too. Stretching was important. You didn't want to pull a muscle or tear anything during practice. But she had to admit it was her least favorite part of this job. She moved to place her feet against Chance's so they could grasp hands and stretch each other's legs and back, but there was a problem.

"This isn't going to work," she said.

His straddle was much wider than her, not only that his legs were way longer. Splits weren't her forte.

"That's because you're not doing it right. Tuck your hips," Chance demanded.

She arched a brow. Chance had always had a bit of a bossy streak. It was one of the things that got under her skin the most. She had no problem listening to people when they were trying to help, but Chance was less helpful and more of a commanding know-it-all.

"Trust me, I know."

See? Know-it-all.

He held up a hand when she let out a harsh laugh at the

very idea. "We're in fake friendship mode right now and I am a personal trainer and certified yoga teacher."

"You are?" Shock held her immobile for half a second. She'd never really contemplated what Chance went off to do after graduation, but those options hadn't been it. She figured the pretty boy who everyone loved would have moved off to Hollywood to become a movie star or something.

He nodded. "I am and if you tuck your hips, it will open up your hip flexors and you can widen your straddle. Try it. Please," he added.

Wow. Now there was a word she never expected to come out of his mouth directed at her. But they were supposed to be getting along, and he did have a good suggestion. Since he backed it up with expertise, she adjusted her seat, tucking her hips. Immediately, she felt her straddle widen, not a lot, but enough that she could press her bare toes against the warm flesh of Chance's heels.

"There you go, you got it," he said with an encouraging smile.

Her lips turned up of their own accord, pride filling her. Achieving a goal always made her happy and increasing her straddle had been on her list for years. Of course it would take her nemesis to help her achieve it.

"Thanks," she said. As much as it begrudged her to admit, he had helped her and he deserved her gratitude.

"Anytime partner."

Ugh, another word she never expected him to direct at her, but here they were. She really needed to make the best of it.

Stretching out her arms, she reached for his hands. The moment his large, warm palms clasped hers, a spark of awareness shot up her arm and ricocheted all throughout her body. She gasped at the sensation, jerking slightly in his hold.

"Iz?" He glanced at her. Concern furrowing his brow. "You okay?"

"Huh?" She shook her head, trying to figure out what the heck that was. "Oh, um, yeah, just…"

"Shit, are my hands too cold?"

He pulled them back, cupping them to his mouth and blowing before vigorously rubbing them together.

"Sorry, I get poor circulation sometimes. Some of my client even call me Frosty the snow hands," he chuckled, reaching out again. "Here. Should be good now."

She hesitated for a moment, then placed her hands back in his. Another zing shot through her, not as strong this time, but still there. Her body warmed at his touch, not froze. Her heartbeat sped up and her blood raced. If she didn't know any better, she'd say she was attracted to Chance.

But she did know better.

There was no way she would ever have the hots for him.

"Okay, I'm going to pull you into the stretch. You tell me when it's good." His face hardened into a mask of concentration; tone slightly stern as he tossed commands at her. "Don't try to save face either. I can't have you injuring yourself before we even get up in the hoop."

She arched a brow at his demand. To his credit he winced slightly, understanding of how his words may have sounded to her entering his eyes.

Clearing his throat, he grinned, giving her a wink and saying with a hint of humor, "I need you to make me look good in there."

She snorted out a chuckle but allowed him to gently pull her into the stretch. Okay, if he was willing to bend so was she. Maybe they could pull off this "fake friend" thing. But she would not be hopping into bed with him, she told her body sternly.

No matter how delicious his arms looked as he flexed, holding her in the stretch. Nope, Chance was off limits. Maybe she needed to get laid. It had been a while. She should take up Tori on her offer to hit the town this weekend. Denver had quite a few LGBTQ+ bars in the city. Tori didn't like crowds, but her bestie enjoyed the bar scene and had been begging Iz to play wingwoman. Maybe they could wingwoman for each other.

Yeah, that was all she needed. A night with her friend blowing off steam and maybe finding a willing partner to hook up with. Nothing serious, seeing as how she'd be leaving on tour soon and needed to end her dry spell before the next one started. Everyone knew that hooking up with someone in your tour was a bad idea—they did it anyway, but it was still not smart.

She smiled as they reversed the stretch. She leveled back up and pulled Chance down for his turn. Her body had calmed, the weird sensations quieting as she planned out her night in her mind. See, it wasn't the man she touched who was setting off all her fuck me hormones. It was simply the fact that she needed some action. And she was going to get it, from someone else, because Iz might have done a lot of stupid things in her life but sleeping with Chance O'Brien would never be one of them.

4

"Hey, you want a beer?"

Chance shook his head, raising his voice so his friend Darnell could hear him about the loud music and din of the bar's patrons. "Naw, I'm good. Water is fine."

Darnell nodded and turned to the bartender to order their drinks. Chance glanced around the crowded bar. Tables and stools lined the outside of the circular room, save for this side which housed a ten-foot-long bar with three people scurrying back and forth, filling orders for the thirsty patrons. In the middle of the room was a large dance floor filled with an array of people moving and dancing to the thumping bass coming from the DJ's speakers. Pride flags and posters littered the wall, letting everyone know this was a safe space.

Bars weren't really his scene, but this place seemed alright and his buddy had been after him for a week now to get out and enjoy the city before he left for his tour. Chance had been lucky that his old college roommate lived in Denver and had been willing to let Chance crash on his couch for the few weeks he'd be in town during the show's rehearsal. Boulder wasn't that far away but making that drive in the Denver traffic every day sounded like a nightmare.

Besides, the lease on his apartment back in Boulder was up so he'd locked up most of his stuff in storage for the next year and taken a sabbatical from his yoga studio. He had no reason to stay in Boulder.

Not after what happened with Ryan.

Shoving off the morose feeling brought up by the thought of his ex, he accepted the water from Darnell when his buddy handed it over.

"So, what do you think?" Darnell asked.

"Kind of loud," he said, raising his voice so his friend could hear him above the music.

Darnell laughed, his locks swaying slightly as he shook his head. "You are such an old man, dude."

"It's not old to want to protect your hearing from eardrum bursting levels of damage."

"Yeah, it is." Darnell took a sip of his drink and pointed to the dance floor. "Get out there. Let loose a little. You got the gig with the show, try to enjoy life a little. Relax."

Relax. A word often spoken to him by everyone in his life. One would think as a yoga instructor, relaxation would be second nature to him. Not true. Meditation was the hardest part of his job. His mind was always running, always focused on the next task.

But was that really a problem? Being driven to accomplish your goals? He didn't think so. If you didn't have goals to work toward, what was even the point of life? His drive helped him achieve the things he wanted in life and if that made him a little...uptight at times, was that really such a bad thing?

Ryan sure thought so.

"You can't control everything and everyone, Chance."

He shook his head. Shoving the negative thought out of his mind. He would not think about his ex anymore. So what if Ryan thought he was a control freak? Control was good. Someone had to be looking out for those around him. Making sure things were getting done. He knew all too well what happened when you left things in the hands of the incapable.

His hand went to the necklace around his neck, rubbing the cool metal engraved with his baby brother's name.

He shook off the dark emotions swimming in his chest, threatening to drown him. Not tonight. Not right now. He was here with his buddy to have fun, blow off steam, and dance. Dropping his hand, he grinned at Darnell.

"Okay, but only if you go with me." Dancing in the air on an apparatus for a crowd of people was one thing. Dancing in the middle of a crowd on the floor was another. One that Chance didn't particularly care for, but his friend was right. He needed to step outside of his comfort zone every once in a while.

"Let's go, dude."

Draining the last of his water, Chance set his glass on the bar and turned to head to the dance floor. But as he turned, he ran smack into someone. Someone small and soft who cursed out his name in a familiar voice.

"Dammit, Chance, can't I get a moment's peace from you?"

He looked down to see peach hair twisted in two space buns and a pair of light brown eyes glaring at him.

"Iz!" He grinned, an unexpected ping of joy hitting him straight in the chest at seeing her adorably grouchy face in front of him. "What a surprise."

"I hate surprises," she grumbled.

Her friend from the show, Tori, if he remembered correctly, was standing next to her, drink in hand. The taller woman gave Iz a gentle shove.

"You're supposed to be playing nice, Iz."

"At the studio, this is a bar."

He chuckled. Her obstinate attitude got him every time. Maybe there was something wrong with him. He loved seeing Iz all feisty and prickly. Leaning down, he gave her a wink and said, "Practice makes perfect."

She rolled her eyes, but he thought he caught a hint of a smile curling the corner of her mouth.

"Iz, Tori, this is Darnell," he said, motioning to his friend as he made introductions. "Darnell, this is Iz and Tori. We're in the show together."

Darnell waved. "Nice to meet you both."

"You too," Tori said with a smile.

"Are you two dating?" Iz asked, fiddling with the label on her beer bottle.

He frowned. What a weird question for her to ask. Normally, Iz didn't want to know anything about him. Why would she ask about his dating life?

"Nope." Darnell smiled. "My boy and I are purely platonic. I'm just here to help him to dip his toe back in the dating game. He's a little gun-shy after his asshole ex. Ryan was such a dick, I don't know what you ever saw in that guy, Chance."

Iz frowned, her gaze snapping to Chance. If he didn't know any better, he'd say there was a hint of sympathy in those brown eyes.

"Asshole ex?"

"Leave it," he muttered to his buddy.

"Dude, he dumped you on the anniversary of your brother's—"

"I said leave it." He glared at his friend. Yes, his ex had dumped him on possibly the worst day of the year, but to Ryan's credit, he hadn't remembered the significance of the day. Because as controlling as Ryan claimed Chance to be, that's how forgetful his ex was. They both had their issues.

Darnell dipped his head, mouthing a small *sorry*.

Louder, to Iz and Tori, Chance explained, "Darnell and I were college roommates. He's been generous enough to let me stay with him during rehearsals until the show tour starts.

"That's nice of you, Darnell, but how are you at wing manning?" Tori motioned to Iz with a shake of her head. "Because this one sucks at it."

"Hey!" Iz protested.

Chance smothered a laugh. He knew people could change, but if Iz was anything like she was in high school, flirting wasn't her game. She liked to pretend he stole all her dates because of his looks and charm—he'd admit those probably helped—but she didn't do herself any favors in the pick-up department. He remembered the time she tried to flirt with the captain of the basketball team and ended up dumping her entire lunch in the poor guy's lap.

"I'm an excellent wingman," Darnell said with a smile. "Just tell me who we're looking for and how I can hype you up."

"Nice!" Tori linked her arm through Darnell's and the two disappeared into the throng of people on the dance floor.

"Did our friends just abandon us?" Iz asked.

"Looks that way."

"Traitors." She frowned, glaring at the dance floor. "So

much for my wingwoman. We were supposed to help each other."

"You looking to hook up, Iz?"

She turned to him, eyes wide. "Not with you."

He shoved down the tiny sting her automatic denial gave him and smiled. "I wasn't suggesting me. I was offering to be *your* wingman."

"Oh."

Her face flushed a bright red. Even in the dim lights of the bar, he could see it spread across her cheeks, darkening the tiny freckles scattered across her nose. Huh, how had he never noticed those before? They were cute. Not a word he normally ascribed to Iz, but he couldn't deny those tiny brown dots gave her a soft look. An observation she wouldn't appreciate him sharing, so he kept it to himself, tucking it away to take out and examine later.

"Never mind, this was a stupid idea anyway." She took a healthy pull from her drink and set the bottle on the bar top. "I don't know why I thought coming to the bar for a hookup was a good idea. I was just trying to distract myself from…"

She trailed off, head turning away from him as she scanned the crowd, but he got the feeling she wasn't looking for anything. More like avoiding him.

"I really shouldn't be out anyway, but Tori is always telling me I need to loosen up."

Darnell's earlier words rang in his ear. Seemed like he and Iz had similar taste in friends.

"What's wrong with being driven?" she continued, pushing on in her one-sided rant. "I mean, really, what is so wrong with having a goal and working toward it?"

He had no idea. "I'm with you. This place isn't bad, but it's loud and crowded and there's a smell in the air that reminds me of gym class and the dumpster behind a burger joint. Honestly, I'd rather be in the studio working on my elbow rolls."

"Exactly!" She turned to him, excitement on her face. "You get it."

He sucked in a breath at the unfiltered joy coming from her smile. He'd never seen Iz smile like that. Not at him, that was for sure. It was beautiful. She was beautiful. He'd always known Iz was attractive in an objective sort of way but seeing such happiness on her face transformed her. It wasn't a look he got to see on her often, or ever really. Something deep inside him ached to see it again.

He shook his head, pushing off the strange feelings her genuine smile stirred in him. Leaning closer, he spoke in a loud mock whisper. "Careful, Iz. I think we just agreed with each other on something."

She snorted. "Hell must have frozen over."

"See?" he said, waving his hand back and forth between them. "We can be friendly."

She rolled her eyes and nodded. "Yeah, I guess so, as long as we're both talking about our overachieving drive to be all work and no fun."

Since they technically weren't competing for anything at the moment, maybe they could use their overachieving drives to their benefit. At least he didn't have to worry about his partner chafing when he requested extra practice. Hell, Iz would probably take his suggestion and double it.

"Stop standing over there like a couple of bar stools and get out here!" Tori called from the edge of the dance floor.

Chance glanced over to see Darnell and Tori had found a couple of willing dance partners and were currently gyrating to the beat of the music. If the smiles on their faces were any indication, they were having a great time.

"Ha! They call that dancing," Iz scoffed. "I bet we could dance circles around them."

There was the Iz he knew, always making things a competition. Only this time it appeared she wanted him with her instead of against her. Could they be forming a friendship? Something he never in a million years thought was possible.

"Oh, we would crush them," he agreed, his competitive drive revving up. "Shall we?"

He held out his hand to her. Iz placed her palm in his. That same tiny shock he felt the other day raced up his arm. He'd assumed it was static from all the equipment in the studio, but clearly it hadn't been. It was Iz.

Ignoring whatever the hell that meant, he pulled her onto the dance floor.

"Holy shit, they're actually here," Darnell said, in shock.

"Don't get too excited," Tori said, spinning her partner into her arms. "Knowing these two, they're probably trying to show us up."

Their friends knew them well, but as the music played and the people around them moved, Chance soon found himself not caring about anything but keeping that bright smile on Iz's face. She twirled around him, moving with him to the beat of the music. Their hands intertwined as they moved around on the dance floor.

It was strange seeing her let loose like this. Even odder was the freedom he felt bubbling up inside him. As they danced, he found himself so in the moment he forgot about everything else. All he could do was feel the beat of the tempo, the press of Iz's soft curves against him.

The music slowed and Iz twirled in his arms; her smile dimming as the people around them swayed sensually to the softer beat. She swallowed, gaze locked on his.

"Um, I think that's good enough." She broke the eye contact. "I think we showed them."

He had no idea. He'd stopped paying attention to showing up their friends because he'd been having too much fun dancing with Iz. Letting loose, as his buddy had suggested.

"I gotta...um, bathroom. See ya at rehearsal, Chance."

Then she was gone, moving through the crowded dance floor, weaving in and out of couples thanks to her small stature. Leaving him standing alone on the dance floor, wondering what the hell just happened.

5

Iz stepped into the studio, a bin of protein bites in hand. They'd been such a hit the other day. Everyone had complimented her on her baking skills and asked if she could bring more. Since baked goods were her love language, she was happy to continue making them. And if it made her popular with her cast-mates, that was a bonus.

A loud laugh carried across the room. She glanced over to see Chance standing with a group of people, animatedly talking as everyone threw their heads back in laughter. Speaking of people with bubbly personalities. Though he was as competitive and driven as her, Chance had always had an easygoing charm about him that drew people in. She admired it as much as she resented it.

Moving to the far wall where they kept the table with the sign-in sheet, sticky spray, and chalk, Iz placed her goodies next to the clipboard and signed in. Memories of dancing with Chance last night invaded her mind as she scribbled her name in dark ink across the lined paper. She never imagined she could have fun with Chance O'Brien—

unless she was kicking his butt in something—but last night had been enjoyable.

Letting loose and dancing with him had been fun, freeing. For once she hadn't felt like she needed to keep up or show him up. They'd simply enjoyed the beat of the music. Until the beat changed, and she'd noticed a few things. Like how close they were. How his large, firm hands felt on her hips. How warm his body had been. The enticing scent of sandalwood that wafted off him, surrounding her like a comforting blanket.

And then the worst thing of all had happened. She felt all the hard ridges of his body pressed up against her and reacted. Or her body reacted anyway. The dimly lit bar had obscured his view of it, but had she not run for the bathroom, he would have felt the way her nipples had pebbled against the thin tank top she'd been wearing last night.

She still couldn't figure out what had happened. Why her body reacted that way. She didn't like Chance on a good day, and she certainly had never been attracted to him.

Liar.

She huffed at her inner bullshit detector. Okay, maybe she'd had one or two hate-fuck fantasies about him over the years, but that didn't mean she wanted to hop into bed with the guy now.

"Hey, Iz," a deep, familiar voice called from behind her.

Speak of the devil.

"You ready for today?"

Taking a fortifying breath, she turned and faced Chance. The smile on his face was open and charming. His brown hair had been pulled back into a bun at the nap of his neck, beard neatly trimmed. The grey sweatpants he had on were tight enough that her horny brain was getting ideas. Or maybe it was his shirtless chest doing that.

Clothing was scarce in the aerial world. The more skin you had to grip on your apparatus, the better. The lack of protective material gave one some nasty bruises, fabric burns, and most lyra performers had rough calluses on their hands. Or, as they more affectionately called them, dick shredders. But it was all for love of the art, so his bare chest shouldn't affect her.

It did.

Her body temperature rose about ten degrees. Throat going dry as she took in all that hewn muscle. The sharp planes and ridges of his pecs and abs entranced her. The dip in his hips, that V shape leading all the way down beneath—

"Iz?"

She shook her head, raising her gaze to his. Heat burned her face, but Chance didn't seem to notice she was standing there basically eye-fucking him. His head tilted, brow furrowed with confusion.

"You okay?"

"Huh? Oh yeah, um what?"

This was ridiculous! Half the people in here were wearing next to nothing. His near nudity shouldn't affect her this way. Usually, Iz herself would be wearing bike shorts and a sports bra. Today she'd gone with full leggings and a tank top. Not because of Chance or these weird feelings he stirred in her. Just because it had been slightly chilly this morning.

It wasn't chilly now. Iz felt like she'd been tossed into an active volcano. All heat and boiling lava surrounding her, ready to explode.

"I asked if you were ready for today?" Chance smiled again, a giddy anticipation filling his eyes. "We're starting rehearsal on our duo act."

Oh right, that. Of course, he had no idea her body was lusting after him of its own accord. *Stupid body*. He was just excited to get in the air. Truth be told, so was she. Now if only she could shove these weird Chance feelings away into a box and toss it in the artic ocean things would be peachy.

"I'm stoked!" She responded, a little too cheerfully if the raise of his eyebrow was any indication. "What size hoop are we using?"

"Jen said she rigged up a 36 inch."

"36?" She frowned. "Isn't that kind of small?"

Barely cresting five-foot, Iz used a 34-inch hoop for solo acts, but with two people, the more room the better. Two more inches hardly seemed like enough room for her and Chance's massive frame.

He shrugged. "I'm sure we can change it to a 38 if the 36 is too small."

She nodded, not sure about anything at this point.

"Let's go warm up."

She followed him through the room, waving to people as they said hi mid-stretch. They made it down to the end of the room where a black untapped hoop hung four feet off the ground. A blue eight-foot mat lay beneath it. Chance moved to the mat and started doing jumping jacks. Iz joined him, following the standard warmup routine Jen and Meg had set out on the first day. They moved through arms, lunges, leg stretches, making their way to back flexibility.

"Partner back arches, people," Jen called out from the center of the room.

Ugh, she hated those. They were great for back flexibility and stretching the shoulders, but they were also damn uncomfortable.

"You wanna go first?" Chance asked, as he rose to his knees.

"Sure." Better to get it over with.

She rolled onto her stomach; arm stretched up above her head. The warm press of Chance's knees cradled her hips as he held himself above her, one leg on either side. He didn't put his weight on her but hovered over. Then his hands were grasping hers, pulling slowing as she leveled her chest up off the mat.

"Tell me when you're good."

She tried to ignore the effect his touch and voice had on her. The tingly sensation running along every nerve. It wasn't Chance. It was simply her body's endorphins responding to the exercise. That was it.

She arched her back, stretching her neck and looking toward the ceiling. The pull of the stretch burned, pinching slightly as he slowly lifted, waiting for her to call it.

"You're going too far, Iz," he warned. "I'm leveling down a bit."

Irritation killed some of the butterflies that had been fluttering low in her belly. Every time she thought they were getting along Chance had to pull out his "I know better" voice and kill the vibe. "I'm fine."

He scoffed. "Pulling a muscle because you overstretched in some weird attempt to prove to me you're more flexible or some shit is a stupid move. I thought we were done competing."

They'd never be done competing. She'd be trying to best Chance until the day she died.

"And I thought you were done being a know-it-all, but here we are."

Chance grumbled something under his breath she couldn't quite make out, then louder, "Sorry. I'm not trying to boss you around. I'm only pointing out that you might want to take it easy on the stretching. I'm...looking out for my partner."

Fine. He had a point, but he could learn to phrase it better instead of insisting he knew her body better than she did.

"Lower half an inch," she grumbled, feeling immediate relief when he did. The stretch was still there, but she didn't feel like her shoulder was about to be ripped from its socket now. "And don't say anything or I will kick your ass."

A chuckle sounded from above her.

"My lips are zipped."

She breathed into the stretch until Meg called out, "Okay, switch it up."

Chance slowly let her arms back down, swing his leg up and over her so Iz could roll over and rise to her knees.

"My turn," he grinned, laying face down in the position she'd just abandoned.

She moved to hover over him the same way he did her, but there was a problem. Once Iz had her knees on either side of his hips, she realized the issue. Her legs were a lot shorter than his, and his hips wider. She'd also been cursed with the flattest ass around while Chance had a backside you could bounce a quarter off of. All this led to the horrifying fact that to properly help him with his stretch, Iz had to rest directly on the man.

Crotch to ass.

"I'm ready," Chance said with utter nonchalance.

At least he didn't seem disturbed by the fact that she was basically riding him like a pony. Or maybe he just understood that this contact would probably be tame compared to what their routine would require them to do. Aerial duo acts required a lot of strange positions and holds that looked pretty, but meant you had to be comfortable being up close and very personal with your partner. Iz needed to get her hormones in check and her head on straight if she was going to get through this.

"Okay, tell me when you're good," she said, reaching up and grabbing his hands. It was tricky considering the height difference, but it amazed her when Chance arched his back, head tilting so she could stare at his upside-down smiling face. "Wow."

"It's the yoga," he said, letting out a long-controlled breath. "Took me years to get this flexible. I can give you some tips if you want."

Old Iz would have scoffed, told him where he could shove it and spent every waking moment practicing on her own so she could wrap herself in a pretzel just to spite him. But she was trying to be more mature, and he had apologized for his earlier command. He was trying too. They had agreed to be friends, and this show was important to her. So, she swallowed her pride and smiled.

"Yeah, that'd be great."

He blinked—a much sillier looking expression when one saw it upside-down—as if he hadn't expected her to agree. She took a small amount of pleasure in that. Maybe surprising Chance would be just as fun as competing with him. Anything that kept him on his toes was a good time in her book.

"Really? Cool."

"And down," Meg called out. "Time for conditioning."

Iz slowly helped lower Chance back to the mat. She released her grip, her fingers slowly stroking the back of his hands of their own accord. She cursed at herself inside and quickly moved off of him. Chance rolled over and pinned her with a stare. She could have sworn she saw a dark flare of heat warming his green eyes, but he blinked, and it disappeared.

"You first again?" he asked, rising, and motioning to their one hoop.

She moved to the hoop and gripped the bottom. "How gentlemanly of you."

"Naw," he grinned. "I'm just waiting to see how many straddle ups you do, so I can do twice as many."

"I thought we weren't competing anymore?"

He winked, the tiny open and close of his eye doing things to her body it had no right to do. She moved her arm to cover her chest, wishing she'd worn her padded sports bra. Hopefully, the tank top would obscure how hard her nipples were right now. From a damn wink!

"Let's think of it as a healthy challenge."

She rolled her eyes, but straddle ups didn't carry the risk of hurting anything like overstretching did. If he wanted to get his butt kicked, she was game. He might have her on the flexibility, but she was the straddle up champion.

"Be prepared to eat crow," she said with a grin, gripping the bar and straightening her legs. "You're about to go down, O'Brien."

6

I z pushed her computer away, stretching her neck and wincing as three loud pops filled the air.

"I've been sitting in this position too long," she said to her empty apartment.

The great thing about being able to work from home was she never had to dress for an office, hit commuter traffic, or make small talk with coworkers. Yuck. The crappy thing was sometimes, when she got in the zone on a project, she forgot to get up and move around. Her muscles cramped as she stood, stretching her arm high above her head. A sigh of relief left her lips right before her stomach made a loud growling noise.

She also forgot to eat.

A quick glance at her laptop showed the time in the top right corner of the screen. One-thirty in the afternoon. No wonder she was hungry. The last meal she'd consumed was her yogurt and granola at seven this morning.

Iz made her way to the kitchen. Since her apartment was a five hundred square foot studio, the kitchen was approximately five feet away from the wall mounted desk where she'd been working. She opened the small single door fridge and peeked at the contents inside. The bright light-bulb in the back of the appliance highlighted the sad fact besides forgetting to eat, Iz had forgotten to go grocery shopping.

A tub of butter, questionable smelling takeout container, and a half empty bottle of wine was all that graced the shelves of her tiny fridge.

"Dining out, it is," she said, closing the door.

Grocery shopping could wait. Everyone knew you didn't go on an empty stomach, or you'd buy the entire store. While her job as a freelance graphic designer paid well enough to keep a roof over her head and support her aerial training, she couldn't afford a massive grocery binge. Besides, she needed to keep her fridge sparse. She'd be going on tour in a few weeks, and she didn't want to come home to spoiled food. Her cousin was coming into town to sublet her apartment for the next year, and their food tastes were exact opposites. No sense in leaving something in the fridge that would sit and rot.

She moved to the front door, slipping her shoes on, and debating if she should change. The black leggings and light blue t-shirt with a printed aerialist on it saying "I fly in the sky, what's your superpower" wasn't exactly the most fash-ionable of outfits, but Iz had never cared much for fashion. She wore what she liked, what felt comfortable. Why cater to what other people like when you're the one who had to live with yourself?

It was also the reason for her choice of hair colors and tattoos. She'd gotten everything from the wide-eyed stares to the mutters of condemnation under a passerby's breath, to outright strangers yelling at her, telling her she was a horrible person for marring her skin. Why the hell did they care so much? It was her skin!

Deciding she felt fine as she was, Iz grabbed her purse and headed out the door. Her apartment was in downtown Denver, located a few blocks from the lower downtown area, or LODO, as the locals called it. The great thing about living in the city was all the amazing places to eat. She contemplated what she felt like eating as she walked down the sidewalk. The bright spring sun warmed her body, loosening up all the cramp muscles that had tightened during her morning power work session.

The client contract she was currently working on was a headache inducer. The guy had hired her to rebrand his entire company. Logos, website, newsletter, everything. He was particular about every little detail, too. She was almost finished with the eighteenth change and if he asked for another, she just might rebrand his face. But he was paying really well and since she needed all the savings she could muster before she headed off on tour, she kept at it. Besides, sometimes the hardest jobs were the most rewarding.

She knew she could still do some work while on tour, but not as much as she usually did, and while the show paid some, it was still the performing arts. The "starving artist" stereotype had come about for a reason.

She turned onto 18th street, glancing up and down at the array of bars, restaurants, coffee shops, and other stores in the area. She still didn't know what she wanted to eat, but the heavenly smells coming from a few of the places down the way called to her. As she made her way toward what her nose determined was a bar-b-que joint, she passed by a familiar shopfront. Reflection Dreams Yoga studio.

Iz paused, glancing into the large glass window lining the front of the shop. She'd taken a few classes here with Tori a year ago. It was a nice studio, clean, calming, with a water feature that bubbled away in the background as the instructors took you through various poses and stretches. Then her schedule had filled, and she had to drop it. Maybe after the show she should take a few more classes. She liked yoga. It helped her stress levels, and she loved the owners. The place didn't look as though it had changed ownership.

She pressed her face closer to the glass, taking in the class currently happening. Yeah, it looked exactly the same as when she'd been. The paint on the walls, the soft, colorful cushions laid around the edge of the room. The group of half a dozen people in downward dog moved, sliding down into cobra position, their stomachs pressed against the floor as they arched their backs.

A gasp left her lips as a familiar face came into view. That was the moment when Iz saw the one thing about the studio that had changed.

The teacher.

There, in the front of the room, revealed now that everyone had moved out of her line of vision, was none other than Chance O'Brien.

"What the hell?"

A few heads turned toward her. Shit! Had she shouted that? Quickly, she ducked back, moving away from the window. She pressed herself against the small bit of brick wall between the front window and the studio door. Crap, had Chance seen her? What the hell was he doing in there, anyway?

Her heart pounded, the heat of embarrassment rising on her cheeks. Did she stay and talk to Chance? Tell him she was just passing by, or did she cut and run? Pretend this never happened?

She was weighing the pros and cons of each scenario when the door to the studio suddenly opened, and people started pouring out. Laughter and conversation filled the air as the students from the class filled the sidewalk where she stood. Some moving away from her down the street, a few passing her with a friendly nod as they headed the other direction. No one said anything about her being a creeper staring into the window. Maybe the glass was opaque enough that they hadn't seen her. She couldn't remember if she'd ever looked out that window when she took classes there.

Maybe this would all go away, and Chance would never—

"Hey Iz, you stalking me now?" A soft chuckle sounded from the open door.

She groaned. Should have known she wouldn't be lucky enough to get out of this one.

"No," she said, turning her head to stare at Chance. The man stood in the doorway, a grin on his face, arms crossed over his naked chest, bare feet poking out of his harem pants. "I was just passing by."

"Passing by the studio I work at?" He raised a brow. "How coincidental."

"I didn't know you worked here," she insisted, her ire rising. "I thought you taught at a studio in Boulder."

"I did, but I'm taking a sabbatical during the tour."

Ha! See, she wasn't a stalker. "Then why are you teaching here?"

"The owner is an old friend. One of the teachers called out sick and since she knew I was in town, she asked me to sub. Trying to save up as much as I can before the tour, you know?"

She did.

"I have a yoga app set up so I can still teach clients remotely on tour, but it won't be like full time or anything so I'm taking any sub gig I can get before we leave."

Made sense.

"Wanna grab some lunch?"

Wait, what? Chance wanted to go to lunch with her? Why? Was he going to poison her or something?

"I'm not trying to poison you," he said with a heavy sigh.

She narrowed her gaze at him. "How did you know I was thinking that?"

"It's you, Iz. You always think the worst of me."

No she didn't. She simply thought he was an arrogant ass who constantly told her what to do and stole everything she worked hard for.

Oh...crap maybe she did. A pinch of guilt wormed its way into her gut. Maybe it was time to give Chance a break.

"I don't want to interrupt any class time." Truthfully, she was still trying to work out if spending time with Chance outside the studio was a good idea. Lately her emotions around this man were all muddled and...strange.

"No worries, I have an hour and a half break until the next class." He grinned down at her. "Think of it as another chance to practice our budding friendship."

Budding fake friendship, but he had a point. The more time they spent trying to get along, the more they actually would, she supposed, and that was good for the show. And for her chances of staying in the show.

"Okay." She pointed to him. "But you better put a shirt and shoes on or nowhere is going to serve us."

They might be in Denver, hipster central, but health code standards still applied.

"Give me one minute."

Chance disappeared into the studio, emerging exactly one minute later with a light grey, V-neck T-shirt on and a pair of flip-flops covering his feet. He locked the studio door, dropping the keys into the pocket of his pants and motioning to the sidewalk.

"Where are we eating?"

She shrugged. "I'm not picky."

"I've been smelling this amazing bar-b-que all day. What do you say we check it out?"

She nodded, not sure if her earlier desire for the same place as him irritated her or helped in their friendship goals.

Fake friendship.

Yeah, they were supposed to be fake friends. Which begged the question; why did Chance seem like he wanted to make it a real friendship? Wariness rose within. What was his game?

Shit, Tori was right. She was too suspicious. Chance had zero reason for messing with her. They weren't competing like they used to. They were both in the show. Both performing on the tour. He had no reason to sabotage her. Unless he was trying to get her kicked out, but that would make him look bad too, working against a fellow performer.

So why the hell was Chance trying to be so chummy with her?

Maybe he really wants to be my friend?

She choked down a laugh at the very thought. Chance O'Brien might want many things from Iz—her humiliation and pride being top among them—but she knew it would be a cold day in hell before he ever truly wanted to be her friend.

"I think I see it, just up there," Chance said, pointing down the street.

"Let's go."

She walked with him down the sidewalk to the restaurant, wondering what game he was playing and how she could beat him at it.

7

W hat the hell had he been thinking?

Chance held the door open for Iz when they reached the restaurant. As she brushed by him, his body tightened with that strange sensation he'd been feeling lately. The one he only experienced when she was in his vicinity. A strange tingle, like his skin was too tight for his body. Maybe he needed to drink more water? Dehydration was no joke, especially when you lived in high elevations like Denver.

He ignored his reaction and followed her inside. He'd invited her along because they were supposed to be playing friendly. For the show. Hopefully, the more they acted like they got along, the more it would become truth and this weird energy that took hold of him every time she was near would go away.

"This place used to be a burger joint," Iz said glancing around at the restaurant. "I haven't been in since it changed ownership."

He'd never been in, but he'd only been in Denver a short while and hadn't explored the city too much.

Glancing around, he noted the place was small. Not claustrophobically, but the restaurant had a dozen tables in the large open room. A small swinging door, which he assumed lead to the kitchen, was in the back left corner. Off to the right was a narrow hallway with a sign hanging above it indicating the way to the bathrooms. The walls of the restaurant were brick, like most of the old buildings in the area, and covered in posters and signage extolling bar-b-que as the end-all-be-all of food.

"Hi there, two?"

Chance turned his gaze to the wooden podium in the middle of the entrance where the host stood. The man smiled at them, the snake bite piercings moving as his lips curled. His short black t-shirt revealed tattooed sleeves in an intricately designed pattern of various anime characters. Black hair pulled back into a bun at the back of his head, much like Chance's.

"Yes, two please," Iz answered, smiling back at the guy.

"Right this way."

The host led them to a table near the front window, setting down their menus.

"Dig your ink," he said to Iz.

Her smile grew as she nodded toward his arms. "Thanks, I like yours too."

"I can give you my artist's number if you want?"

She laughed softly, the sound hitting Chance low in the gut. He shifted in his seat as he watched their host flirt with her. He didn't blame the guy. Iz was beautiful. Like one of those poison dart frogs, all pretty and innocent looking until you tried to touch them then, BAM, death. Or maybe she was just that way with him.

"Thanks, but I can't cheat on my tattoo artist. She's the best."

The host nodded knowingly. "Fair. Your server will be right out. Enjoy."

The host left, leaving them alone. A few of the other tables were occupied by couples, groups, and one family with a toddler who was eating more sauce than meat. None of the tables near them had people at them, which left them relatively alone in their space.

"I think he likes you," Chance said, opening his menu and nodding to where the host was standing at his podium.

"Naw, he was just admiring my ink." Iz snorted. "Besides, he's not my type."

Really? Seemed like a tatted-up alt guy would fit Iz's aesthetic perfectly. Why that thought sent a sharp pang of irritation through him he had no idea.

"I can't date someone who has more tattoos than me." She winked.

He chuckled. "Gotta be the best?"

"Always."

She lifted her water glass, and he raised his own to clink.

"Maybe I'll ask for his number then," he said, taking a sip of the cold, iced water. "He's cute."

Her brow arched. "You think you could get his number before I can?"

He felt his lips curve up in a grin. A tiny flame sparking to life. The one he always got when facing off against this dynamic woman in front of him. She challenged him like no one else, and he wasn't above admitting he liked it. Facing off against Iz was like a drug, addicting.

"I mean, yeah."

"In your dreams," she tossed back at him.

"Who got to take Kelly to prom again? Who was that?" He tapped his chin with a finger. "Oh right, me. She picked me over you."

Fire burned in her brown eyes, one that promised retribution. "Only because you promised her you'd rent a limo."

"And because of my devastating good looks." He winked.

"Oh, that's how you want to play this? Fine, first one to get the host's number—"

Her words died as a tall redhead with gauged ears came in the front door, headed right to the host stand and wrapped her arms around the guy, planting a very not safe for work kiss on his mouth.

"Oh, um, never mind," Iz muttered. "See, I told you he wasn't flirting."

As if she would ever know. Iz was terrible at social cues. She always had been. Which was the real reason Kelly accepted his promposal over Iz's. He'd asked with a dozen roses, a sign with a pun on it. According to Kelly, Iz had mumbled something about going to prom together and rushed off. Kelly hadn't even been sure it was a promposal.

Poor Iz. Wasn't her fault he had more charm than her. Still, he was glad he'd been wrong about the host. Not that he begrudged Iz and any hookup she wanted to partake in, but something about competing with her for a date didn't sit right. Didn't feel as fun as it used to. Maybe they were maturing. Or maybe he didn't like the thought of Iz with someone else.

He snorted. What a ridiculous notion that was. Why would he care if Iz was with someone else? What did he expect...her to be with him?

The thought made him pause.

He'd be lying if he said he hadn't entertained a fantasy or two of him and Iz together over the years, but it was mostly one of those hot bang-your-enemy type things. He never actually believed they would be a good match.

They'd likely kill each other before kissing each other.

He laughed inside, shaking his head, pushing the ludicrous thoughts away. This whole "get along with Iz" thing was messing with him.

"Hi there."

A bubbly voice interrupted his thoughts. He glanced up to see a tall woman with long box braids gathered in a low ponytail and a bright smile on her face.

"Welcome to Bernie's Bar-B-Que, I'm your server Bree. What can I get started for you?"

He nodded to Iz, who waved a hand in the air.

"You first, I'm still deciding."

"I'll have the pulled pork sandwich with fries, please."

Bree nodded, writing his order on the pad in her hand. "And what level of heat would you like the sauce on that? Mild, hot, or fire?"

"Hot please."

She nodded, noting his preference before turning her attention to Iz. "And for you?"

"The same, please." She shifted her gaze to him, the corner of her mouth curling up in a devilish smile. "But fire sauce for me."

He shook his head as Bree left to put in their order.

"Seriously, did you just order a hotter sauce to show me up?"

She shrugged. "Hey if you can't handle a little spice, it's none of my business."

He rolled his lips in to keep from laughing. She would do anything to beat him. At least she seemed to be playing semi-nice. She hadn't threatened him with bodily harm yet, so he was calling it a win. Maybe they could be friends, real friends.

"So, how's your family?"

Her lips rolled in at his question, the corner of her mouth quirking up. "Really? Small talk?"

He shrugged. "We're supposed to be getting along, friendly. Friends engage in small talk about life and things like family."

She sighed, head shaking as if he were the most annoying person on the planet. To her, he probably was. The thought made him grin.

"They're fine. My sister married some guy she met in dental school. They moved to Montana and have a practice out there and two adorable little boys who take after their perfect aunt." She smiled, love for her nephews shining clearly in her eyes. "My mom lives next door and loves being grandma on call 24/7."

He remembered her older sister a bit. She was two grades ahead of him and Iz, so he didn't really know her, but he knew she and Iz were tight. Since he wasn't what one would call friendly with the Grant girls, he didn't know much about Iz's home life, but he had heard through school gossip that Iz's dad ran out on them when Iz had been in kindergarten, leaving her mom to shoulder everything.

Shitty thing to do. And he knew shitty parents. His hadn't abandoned him like that, but there was more than one way to be an absent parent and his sure found a way to not be there while still physically being there.

"How about you?" She asked. "How's your family?"

Shit! He hadn't thought this one through when he started. Of course, a part of being friendly was reciprocating. He asked about her family, so it was only natural for her to ask about his. Something he never discussed. Even in school, he hadn't liked talking about his home life.

"You have a younger brother, right?" Iz asked, tilting her head. "How's he doing these days?"

Chance swallowed hard. The sharp stab of pain when he thought about Cameron pinching his chest. It never went away. Some days it wasn't as piercing as others, but it was always there. The hurt, the loss, the guilt.

He hated talking about his brother. The pain it brought up, the anger at his parents, the anger at himself for failing Cameron when he needed his big brother most. Chance had tried so hard, but it hadn't been enough. He hadn't been enough. A regret he would shoulder until his dying day.

"Chance?"

He glanced up to see Iz staring at him with a concerned expression. Shit. He'd been silent too long. Wallowing in his misery, his past failings. She asked about his family, but what the hell could he tell her? His alcoholic parents neglected them so much that when his brother got sick, they didn't even realize or do anything until it was too late? Yeah, that was real cheery lunch conversation.

"Oh hey," he said, turning his head to the side and glancing out the window and pointing. "Isn't that Tori?"

"What?" Iz's brow furrowed as she turned and looked at where he pointed.

It wasn't Tori. In fact, there wasn't anyone walking along the sidewalk right now. He'd just panicked. Dammit, why had he thought this lunch was a good idea again?

Iz's head swung back his way. She frowned, hand reaching across the table. "Chance, if you don't want to talk about—"

"And lunch is served!"

Chance breathed a sigh of relief as Bree arrived at the table, two plates in hand, and set them down. Saved by the server. Iz pulled her hand back into her lap. Concern and a pinch of irritation lighting her eyes as she stared at him.

"Do you all need anything else right now?"

"No, thanks." He pasted on the brightest smile he could muster. "This is great."

Bree nodded and left.

Chance grabbed his sandwich and took a big bite. Couldn't talk about his family if his mouth was full. That would just be rude. He glanced over to see Iz still staring. Her brow was furrowed, and that damn concern wouldn't leave her eyes. Why the hell had he brought up family? He'd rather talk about his dick of an ex.

Deciding to take the cowards way out and not talk about anything personal, he nodded to her food.

He nodded to her food. "You chickening out, Iz?"

A small sigh left her lips as she accepted his refusal to talk about what was bothering him, but she said nothing. Simply grabbed her sandwich with both hands using a hold that ensured both her middle fingers were on top of the bun and facing him as she took a large bite.

He held his sandwich in front of his mouth as a chuckle escaped.

She chewed, eyes widening, the angry furrow in her brow morphing into one of worry. Round eyes blinked, moisture gathering in the corners as she sucked in deep breaths, her nostrils flaring.

"Iz?" He put his sandwich down and leaned forward. "You okay?"

His sandwich packed quite the spicy punch. He could only imagine how much hotter hers was.

"I'm fine," the words squeaked out of her throat.

"Spicy food has been known to cause damage to the body. You can burn your esophagus, get an ulcer. I think you should ask the server for some milk to cut back on the heat."

"Oh, you think so, do you?" With a defiant glare, she

lifted the sandwich and took another ill-advised massive bite.

"Mmmmm," she mumbled around the food filling her cheeks.

Though it sounded more like a moan of pain than pleasure to him.

"So...good," she panted out after she swallowed the bite. Grabbing her water and downing half the glass. "Really... really...good. But I forgot I had such a big breakfast. I think I'll just eat my fries and take the sandwich home for later."

He smothered his laughter by taking another bite of his own lunch. Of course she'd do the exact opposite of what he said. Classic Iz.

They finished their meal, sticking to conversations about the show and how excited they were to travel. Thankfully, she let his refusal to talk about his family go. After they paid, they left the restaurant, walking back toward the yoga studio.

"I should get back to work," Iz said as they arrived at the front door.

"Yeah, I have another class to teach in half an hour. Thanks for joining me for lunch. Hope you didn't burn all your taste buds off."

"Stuff it, Chance," she grumbled, but there was little heat to it.

He laughed. "Okay, you enjoy that sandwich later. Maybe keep a gallon of milk near you just in case."

"You are so annoying." She rolled her eyes, giving him a playful shove.

He had no idea what possessed him to do it, but he grabbed her arm, tugging her into him. "Only because you're so fun to annoy."

She sucked in a sharp breath as one hand landed on his

chest. He could feel the warmth of her palm against the pounding of his heart. Could she feel how fast it was beating? Did she know why? Hell, he didn't even know why!

A quick glance into her eyes and he called himself a liar.

He knew exactly why.

Heat flared in those dark brown depths. The same heat he knew was in his own. The same heat he felt low in his gut every time this woman was near him.

Fuck!

He was attracted to Izadora Grant.

8

Iz popped a caffeine mint into her mouth as she entered the aerial studio. The candy was an easy way to get a wake-up jolt and much more practical since she was about to head into rehearsal. Spinning in the air with a belly full of coffee was a sure way to repaint the studio floor with her dinner.

She'd slept like crap last night. All thanks to a certain man with a smart-ass grin, tempting rock-hard body, and the ability to annoy the ever-living hell out of her. Going to lunch yesterday with Chance had been a huge mistake. First because she had to spend time with him. She was getting used to being around him. Which was good, she supposed, since they had to work together, but she had to wonder if getting *too* close to Chance was a good idea?

Being friendly was one thing, but when she asked about his family... She'd only been trying to be polite. He asked her first, it was only natural for her to ask him. She had no idea it would cause him to close off like that. Honestly, she wasn't even sure what happened, but she recognized pain and it been coming off Chance in waves when she mentioned his brother. Her heart ached at the haunted look she'd spotted in his eyes. A desperate need to ask, to comfort, had risen in her, but Chance made it abundantly clear he didn't want to talk about whatever had turned his mood, so she'd let it drop.

Still, she wondered what dark pain could have caused such a shift in the normally bright and sunny man. It wasn't like Chance at all and it...worried her. She never imagined she'd be worrying about Chance O'Brien, but the more time they spent together the more he wormed his way into her thoughts.

But the thing that really had her tossing and turning all night long was the moment where he pulled her into him. The moment she couldn't stop playing over and over again in her mind. His teasing grin, the warmth of his body, the rapid beat of his heart when she placed her hand on his chest, and the heat that flared in his eyes.

Iz wasn't as socially ignorant as everyone thought her to be. Yes, she was a little blunt, some people might say rude. She couldn't flirt to save her life and most of her past relationships had crashed and burned. Still, she knew when someone was attracted to her and the hungry look on Chance's face yesterday hadn't been directed at her leftovers.

Normally, it wouldn't be a problem. Hell, a few years ago she'd even get a kick out of her nemesis having the hots for her. But there was one major, horrifying problem...

She had the hots for him too.

Regrettably, Iz couldn't deny the fact that she found Chance attractive. Her body reacted every time he was near. Her heart raced, nipples stiffened, heat and moisture gathered between her thighs, and it was all she could do to stop herself from grabbing the man and climbing him like a tree.

A terrible option, considering they didn't even like each other.

She sighed as she moved to the table and put her name on the sign-in sheet. Okay, so maybe they were starting to get along. A little. But that didn't mean it was a good idea, or a wise one, to hop into bed with the guy. Hooking up with someone else wasn't an option either. She'd tried to go out with Tori to the bar again, but no one caught her interest.

Damn you, Chance O'Brien!

This was all his fault somehow. He'd cast a sexy lust spell over her or something. That was ridiculous, but she didn't have any other explanation for the sudden attraction to the man.

"Okay everyone, listen up," Jen called from the center of the room. "We're working on the duo acts today, so find your partner and warm up."

Iz screamed internally. Yes, she knew from the schedule they were working on the duo acts, but she'd been hoping by some miracle of mix up she'd arrive to discover they were doing the groups acts. No such luck.

The hoop for her and Chance's act was set up in the back of the studio. Iz stuffed her shoes and bag in a cubby, grabbing her water bottle, and headed over to the mat under the hoop where Chance was warming up.

"Hey, Dragon, how's it going?"

She frowned, "Huh?"

"You know," he winked, giving her a smart-ass grin. "Because you like to eat fire."

She didn't know whether to be annoyed or relieved that yesterday's incident didn't seem to have as much of an effect on him as it had on her. On the one hand, she was thankful there would be no weird tension between them today, but on the other she couldn't squelch the irritation that she stayed up all last night having sexual fantasies about the man, and he appeared to have slept like a baby.

She glanced over her shoulder quickly to make sure Meg and Jen weren't watching, then turned back to him and lifted a middle finger, kissing it and blowing it his way. Chance laughed.

Confidence calmed Iz's nerves as they warmed up. The familiar routine of the exercises settling her. The weirdness she felt around Chance moved to the back of her mind as her body took over, stretching, bending, and prepping for the workout she was about to give it. Once warmups were done, Jen came over to their mat for instructions.

And that's when everything fell apart.

As Jen took them through the routine, teaching them the first half, Iz's body lost its calm. The moves weren't difficult —most of them anyway—but every time she had to touch Chance her body went into overdrive. Sparks shot up her spine, heat burned her cheeks, tiny tremors danced along every muscle making her jerk, mess up the moves.

"Okay, hold up," Jen said, as they messed up yet another move.

Iz dropped from the position she was in under the bar. It was a simple move. All she had to do was grab the bar, kick her foot up into Chance's hold and rotate her body into Peter Pan pose. It wasn't that hard! She'd done it a million times with Tori. So why was her body refusing to turn the right way?

She held back a frustrated scream as Jen came over to her side.

"You okay today, Iz?"

The tall woman was so nice. Yes, she was technically the boss, but Jen and Meg cared about the performers. Still, Iz wasn't about to tell her boss she couldn't get a basic ass move because she wanted to jump her partner's bones.

"Yes, I'm sorry Jen. I...I didn't sleep well last night, and I think it's making my brain fuzzy. I'm so sorry. I promise I can get this."

Jen grabbed her hand and gave a reassuring squeeze. "It's okay, Iz. We all have off days. Besides, this is what rehearsal is for, to work out the kinks. Why don't we call it for the night? You know the moves and can work on them next time. Have some chamomile tea before bed tonight. It'll help you sleep."

She nodded as the aerial show owner smiled and headed over to another duo act that was working with Meg. Iz sucked in a deep breath, frustrated tears threatening to fall, but she blinked them back. She hated failing. Even if it was inevitable in life, it still sucked.

A thump sounded beside her, and she turned to see Chance standing on the mat beside her. He must have hopped down from his position in the hoop. His face filled with the same frustration she felt. Arms crossing over his chest as he frowned at her.

"You're turning the wrong way. You have to go right not left. Move toward the hand on the bar, rotate your shoulder."

"I know that." She glared at him. She didn't need Mr. Know-it-all pointing out things she already knew.

He held up his hands huffing out an exasperated breath. "I'm just trying to help."

No, he was bossing her around like always.

"What's up, Iz?"

At the moment? Her ability to deal with him.

"Nothing, I'm just tired."

Needing to get some fresh air, air that didn't involve her

breathing in Chance's tempting scent with each inhale, she hurried over to the cubbies and grabbed her stuff. Slipping on her shoes, she booked it out of the studio and into the cool spring night air. She made it all the way to her car before she heard the fall of heavy footsteps behind her.

"Iz, wait up!"

Ugh! Could the man not see she needed space from him right now? What was with him? Maybe he was doing this on purpose. Making himself all sexy and irresistible to mess with her head so she'd screw up the moves and get kicked out of the show. The thought made her blood boil. Irrational thought took over. She whirled around, nearly smacking right into Chance as he invaded her personal space.

"What the hell is wrong with you?"

His eyebrows climbed up his forehead. "Me?"

"Yes, you." A snarl left her.

"You're the one who rushed out of the studio like your ass was on fire."

To get away from him.

"Maybe that was a hint that I wanted to be left alone."

"Come on, Iz." He gently gripped her arm, tugging her closer as he stared into her eyes. "Talk to me."

Her heart skipped a beat at the touch. A sharp throb pulsing between her legs at the soft brush of his skin against hers. She pushed down the unwanted sensation, reaching for her anger, wishing the familiar emotion would take over this newer one she had no idea what to do with.

"You want me to talk to you?" She raised one eyebrow.

Chance nodded. "Yeah, we're supposed to be acting like friends now and that's what friends do.

A harsh laugh escaped her. "Friends? If we're such good friends, why don't you share with me? Huh?"

"What the hell is that supposed to mean?"

"You want me to share, but the other day at lunch when I asked about your family, you pulled a sitcom worthy distraction bit to avoid sharing a single word."

She could still remember the brief moment of pain that flashed in his eyes when she'd asked about his brother. Something inside her wouldn't let it go. Wouldn't let her forget. Some driving need within her urged her to do everything in her power to help erase that look of bleak misery from his eyes forever. But she couldn't do that even if she wanted to. The damn man shared advice like it was going out of business, but kept his personal life locked in a freaking vault. Why was she expected to share when he wouldn't?

He dropped her arm, taking a small step back, gaze falling to the ground. "That's...different."

"How?"

His jaw tightened, eyes still refusing to meet hers as he shrugged. "It just is. Now tell me why you left the studio in such a hurry."

This man made her so frustrated she could scream. But since she didn't want to draw the attention of anyone still left in the studio, she settled for a low growl.

"Maybe I was tired of being dictated to by my supposed partner."

"I was helping," he insisted.

"I didn't ask for your help, Chance!"

Chance leaned back, crossing his arms over his chest. "Fine! I just came out to check on you. Excuse the hell out of me for caring about my duo partner."

"I don't need checking on. I'm fine."

He snorted. "Really? Then how come every time I grabbed you for a hold you flinched?"

She sucked in a sharp breath. He felt that? Fuck, of

course he did. His hands had been all over her tonight as they learned the routine. He'd have to be a terrible aerialist not to notice what his partner's body was doing so up close and personal. And as much as it pained her to admit, Chance was an extremely good aerialist.

"You are so annoying," she threw at him.

"And you're deflecting," he countered. "Now what the hell was up tonight? What did I do?"

She paused, taking in his question, staring into his face. His...worried face. Dammit, Chance thought he was the cause of her fuckups tonight. He was, but not in the way he meant. As frustrated as she was with him right now, she couldn't let him think her failing was his fault. That wasn't fair.

"It's not you. It...I'm tired." She turned, grabbing her keys from her bag. "I just want to go home."

"Iz, talk to me."

She held back a growl. Why wouldn't he let it go? Let her go? All she wanted to do was go home, break out her vibrator and work out this unwanted sexual attraction she had to the man in the privacy of her own home. It hadn't worked last night, but maybe she needed a few more orgasms to sate her body, and then she could forget all about Chance O'Brien and the way he made her thighs clench. If she orgasmed herself into exhaustion, that had to work, right?

"Iz!" He insisted, gently grasping her arm.

That was it! Her nerves were done, she couldn't do it. Whirling around, her mouth opened, and she exploded her tension, frustration, and confusion all over him.

"You wanna know what happened tonight? You, okay! You happened. I couldn't focus on what I was supposed to do, how I was supposed to turn, where to put my hands, because the second you touch me, all I want to do is put my hands all over you! I want to take you down to that mat, rip off all our clothes and fuck you until neither of us can walk straight let alone perform out routine. So there, that's what happened tonight. My stupid horny brain took over because apparently, against all my better judgment, I suddenly want to have sex with you."

She sucked in deep, heaving breaths as her rant ended. Chance stood there, slack jawed, staring at her with a mix of shock and something else...

Hunger.

"You want to have sex with me?" he said slowly, the words rumbling deeply out from his lips.

"I know. Hell must have frozen over."

He grinned at her barb, stepping closer until he was inches from her. She could feel the warmth of his breath against her cheek as he leaned down to whisper in her ear.

"Then it must have frozen over twice because I sure as hell want to fuck you, too."

She pulled back, excitement and wariness warring within her as she glanced up into his eyes. "But we won't because it's a bad idea, right?"

"Colossally bad," he agreed, dipping his head closer until their lips were a hairsbreadth apart.

"And we don't want to do anything to mess up this opportunity." She moved her own head a millimeter closer, her lips barely brushing against his as she spoke.

"Yes, but what's worse? Ignoring this attraction and letting it fester, causing us to gripe at each other and fail in rehearsal."

That sounded miserable, and like a surefire way to get booted from her dream job.

"Or," he said, grasping her hips and tugging her flush

against him until she could feel the hard length of his erection against her stomach, "we get rid of whatever this thing we stepped into is."

"Are you suggesting we fuck away our attraction, Chance?"

He brushed his lips against hers, tempting her with the promise of what they could give, while teasing her, pulling away just before she could truly taste how sinfully good he was.

"That is exactly what I'm suggesting."

9

"Get your car, follow me."

Chance nodded silently to Iz, but inside he was shouting in celebration. Was this a bad idea? Possibly. Did he care? Not in the slightest. Truth be told, he'd had a thing for Iz since high school, but she'd always been more determined to bite his head off rather than hold his hand, so he pushed the attraction down deep. Refusing to recognize it. But now...

Now she wanted him.

No way was he going to pass up this opportunity. Besides, they couldn't keep going like this. Sniping at each other during rehearsal. Maybe finally getting this strange lustful attraction out of their system would be a good thing and they could work on being real friends after.

Or it could all blow up in their faces.

He hurried to his car, starting it up and following Iz out of the parking lot. They didn't discuss where they were going, but he assumed her place since she commanded him to follow her. They sure as shit couldn't go to his place considering he was sleeping on Darnell's couch right now. Hopefully, Iz didn't have a roommate.

He followed her tiny blue car down the hard to navigate one-way streets of the city until she pulled into a parking lot of an apartment building. Chance saw an open spot on the street right in front and slid into it. He hurried out of his car, locking the doors before rushing to the front of the building where Iz waited, bouncing on her toes as he approached.

"I'm on the first floor. Come on."

No time for sweet talk, he supposed. That was fine. He didn't need any preamble, he needed her. His skin felt too tight, like he was about to burst if he didn't do something soon. The something being the short, sexy woman he was currently following through the building's front door.

Iz lead them down a hallway, stopping almost at the end and slipping a key into the door. She pushed it open, moving through it without looking back. She knew he'd follow. Normally, her smugness would cause him to act the exact opposite of what she expected, but not tonight. Tonight, for the first time ever, they wanted the same thing. He was only too happy to follow someone else's demands for a change.

He stepped into her place, noticing how Iz-like it looked right away. It was small, a studio with a tiny couch in the center of the room, a small flatscreen on the wall, a bed in the corner, and a kitchen area with a tiny dining set off to the side. There was also a door to his right, which he assumed led to a bathroom, the only room in the place. The size wasn't the only thing that resembled Iz. Every inch of the place was filled with bright colors.

The couch was sky blue with glittery silver stripes. The bedspread was a blinding bright yellow, and half a dozen throw pillows of various colors and patterns scattered about the place.

"Nice place." He grinned down at her, leaning against the closed door.

"We don't need small talk, Chance."

"What, I can't comment on your interior decorating skills?" He chuckled softly.

She rolled her eyes. "Do you want to talk or fuck?"

Then she reached for the hem of her tank top and in a move more impressive than he would ever admit to her, she pulled off her shirt and sports bra in one fell swoop. His laughter died, mouthwatering as he took in her breasts. They were perfection. Small and beautiful, with dusky rose nipples that hardened into stiff peaks as he stared.

"Fuck, please."

He moved toward her, dropping his hands to her waist, and pulling her into him. A knowing grin curved her lips. She placed her hands on his shoulders. He arched one eyebrow in question, and she nodded. Dipping his head, he brushed his lips over one pert nipple. Iz moaned, the sound going straight to his dick. He was so hard it hurt, but he wasn't about to rush this. Not with her.

He parted his lips, pulling her nipple into his mouth and swirling his tongue around the stiff bud. Iz cried out, her hands moving up his shoulders and neck, into his hair. She grasped the strands, the motion causing his bun to loosen slightly. He didn't care. She could rip every single strand from his head if it meant he got to keep savoring her. She tasted like sunshine and electricity, heaven and danger all wrapped up into one.

She tugged his head close, and he obliged. Biting down softly, drawing a keening cry from her lips. The sound echoed inside him, spurring him on as he moved his hands up, sliding them up her rib cage, reveling in the softness of her skin. He brushed the underside of her breasts with his thumbs, drawing another sweet moan. Damn, he could find himself addicted to those noises she made.

He glided his lips along her skin, giving her chest soft kisses as he focused on her other breast. Lavishing it with the same care and attention he did the first.

"Chance," she panted, her body pressing against his. "Please."

Abandoning her magnificent breasts, he continued down her body, placing hungry love bites along her stomach until he got to the waistband of her leggings. Hooking a finger at each hip, he pulled the garment down, along with her underwear. Iz quickly stepped out of them, widening her stance as he dropped to his knees.

Chance stared at the sight before him. The small thatch of pale blonde curls covering the part of her he craved most.

"Open for me, Iz." He glanced up at her. "Please."

She stared down at him, no longer looking smug, but needy. There was a hungry, desperate look in her eyes, and he planned to sate it. Over and over again. She started to move her leg to the side, then with a wicked smile, she lifted it and placed her thigh on his shoulder. He grinned up at her. When she raised a brow in challenge, he growled. Grasping her other leg, he tugged, lifting her and placing it over his free shoulder. The position had her back flat against the wall, weight supported by it and him.

He grasped her hips with his hands and tugged her closer, his nose brushing her curls. A deep inhale had her intoxicating scent driving him wild. His fingers tightened on her as he tilted her hips to give him the perfect angle, swiping out his tongue in one long, broad stroke as he tasted her. Iz cried out above him, her thighs squeezing his head.

He devoured her, circling her clit, thrusting inside, listing to her sounds and adjusting to what she liked. Before long she was crying out, coming against his face and he couldn't get enough.

"Holy fuck, Chance," she panted, legs giving out as she sagged against him and the wall.

"We're not done yet." His cock was so hard he feared he might rip right through his pants.

"Damn right we aren't."

He felt the gentle brush of heated skin as her legs slid off his shoulders. He rose from his kneeling position to stand in front of her. Her eyes stared straight into his as she reached out a hand grasping his cock through the thin cotton work out pants he wore. He hissed, the touch soothing and torture at the same time.

Her warm breath electrified his every nerve ending as she got up on her toes and whispered in his ear, "Lose the clothes and come to the bed."

He damn near cried like a baby when she let him go but watching her spectacular naked ass as she sauntered across the room to the bed made up for the loss of her touch. Faster than he thought possible, Chance stripped all his clothing off and hurried to her. Iz reached into the nightstand by the bed and pulled out a box of condoms. She took one out and turned to him, gaze falling to his jutting erection.

"Mmmm." Her sweet pink tongue came out to swipe across her lower lip. "Maybe I should have a taste before we—"

"No." He grabbed the condom from her, ripping open the package and rolling it on. "Later. Right now, I need to be inside you."

She chuckled. "Eager?"

Reaching down, he slipped two fingers into her heat. She clenched around him, letting out a soft moan. "You aren't?"

"Shut up and fuck me, Chance."

"As you wish."

He turned her, pressing down on her shoulders. Iz followed his command, placing her hands on the bed and spreading her legs, wiggling that tight little ass in the air. He damn near lost it, but he managed to keep his control. Grabbing her hips, he pulled her to him, placing his cock at her entrance.

"Ready?"

"Now!" she demanded.

He chuckled, his laughter turning into a loud moan as he thrust inside her. Fuck! Nothing had ever felt so good. She called out his name, pressing back against him. Taking him deeper. After his body adjusted to the shock, he set a steady pace, holding her hips as he drove into her.

"Chance...I need..."

He knew what she needed. Reaching around with one hand, he found her clit, circling with just the right amount of pressure he'd already learned she loved. She cried out, demanding he give her more, faster, harder. Fuck, he never thought he'd enjoy Iz telling him what to do, but all he wanted to do was agree to her every demand right now. He felt his body tighten, but he'd be damned if he came before her. Increasing the pressure, he tilted her hips, the new position causing him to go even deeper. Iz cried out, her walls tightening around his cock, milking him as her orgasm hit. He allowed himself to let go then. Losing himself inside her.

They collapsed on the bed. He rolled them onto their sides so he didn't crush her. His breath coming in heavy pants, hers matching as they both came down from the amazing ride.

"Fuck me, that was amazing," she said.

He kissed her neck, the soft spot right below her ear. "Thanks, I'm pretty proud of myself, too."

She glared at him over her shoulder. "Proud of *yourself*?"

He grinned. "Yeah. I mean, I gave you two orgasms. That means I win, right?"

One brow arched. "Are we competing for orgasms? Because that's really not fair. Women can have more in one night than men."

"Oh, can they?" He met her arched brow, already feeling himself grow hard in her again.

A second eyebrow joined her first before a mischievous smile crossed her lips. "If we're competing for orgasms, then it's a good thing I have an entire box of condoms, isn't it?"

He grinned, kissing her lips softly as he whispered, "A very good thing. May the best lover win."

"Oh," she nipped at his lip as he pulled away. "I plan to."

10

Iz woke up feeling better than she had in weeks. A smile curled her lips as she rolled over in her bed, snuggling deeper into the warm, cozy blankets. She couldn't remember the last time she'd slept that well. Chance was like a dose of sexual melatonin.

"Morning."

She cracked an eye open at the deep cheery voice, spying Chance standing in nothing but his boxers at her kitchen counter, sipping from a steaming mug. Holding the blanket to her chest because she was still naked—yes, he'd seen and touched everything last night, but in the light of day it was...different—she sat up and frowned.

"You're still here."

He paused, placing his mug on the counter. "Am I not supposed to be?"

She shrugged. They hadn't really discussed what came after. She'd been so out of her mind with need last night. This thing had been a whim, and then they'd both fallen into an exhausted sleep.

"I, um, kind of figured you would have snuck out while I was sleeping."

He cocked his head. "A lot of your hookups do that to you?"

She shrugged as if it didn't sting each time it happened. "A few."

"Hm, that's shitty. You deserve better, Iz."

She ducked her head to hide a smile. "Yeah, well, don't expect me to make you breakfast in bed or anything."

"I'm not in bed," he said with a grin. "You are. So, what'll it be?"

He was going to cook her breakfast? Who the hell was Chance O'Brien, really?

It wasn't fair of her to make assumptions about the man's dating style. Not that they were dating. They weren't. They just hooked up. Once. But she never expected him to be the stick around, make breakfast kind of guy. Or maybe that was simply her presumptions about the man because she'd disliked him for so long.

"You can cook, right?" She narrowed her eyes, suspicion clouding her voice. "This isn't some long con to burn my kitchen down or anything, is it?"

He laughed, shaking his head as he moved to her refrigerator. "So suspicious, Iz."

Of him? Always.

Just because they had sex didn't mean she was ready to move him into the trustworthy category of her life. They had years of messing with each other behind them. A few amazing orgasms did not erase history like that.

"Why do you have nothing but expired milk and butter in here?"

"I don't eat a lot of meals at home. Cooking for one is... not really worth it." She made plenty of baked good for her friends at the studio but cooking for herself felt kind of...lonely.

"You don't cook at all, it seems. It's not healthy to eat out every meal, Iz. You should really think about what you put into your body. Junk food every now and then is okay but eating out for every meal isn't good for you."

A growl escaped her as irritation burned in her chest. There was the Chance she knew, the guy who thought he knew best. So nice of him to show his head again and remind her why this had been a one and done type deal.

Tossing back the covers, she grabbed her robe from the hook on the wall and covered herself. Tying the knot tighter than necessary, she scooped up Chance's clothing from the night before that were scattered all over her floor.

"Here," she said, shoving the bundle against his chest. "Get dressed and get out."

"You're kicking me out?" he asked with an arched brow.

"We're done here and as you said, I have no food for you to cook so there's no reason for you to stay."

His gaze flittered over her shoulder to the bed in the corner and back to her. "So...that's it? It's out of our system? Just one night, is it?"

She nodded. "Yup. I think we're good."

Her body screamed, calling her a liar. One and done was not going to satisfy her. She wanted Chance again and again. Which was why she was kicking him out. A fun night in the sack was one thing but getting involved with him would be a terrible idea.

He stood there, gaze searching her face for endless minutes. Finally, he shrugged and started pulling his clothing on.

"Okay, I guess. Sure I can't take you out for breakfast? You gotta eat, Iz."

What was with his obsession with her diet this morning?

"I have protein shakes in the cupboard. I have to get some work done before rehearsal anyway, so, thanks for the orgasms and see you tonight."

He made a half laugh, half grunt sound as she practically pushed him out the door.

"You're welcome I guess, but shouldn't we talk about—"

The rest of his words were muffled as she shut the door in his face, calling out, "Bye, Chance."

"Bye, Iz." His farewell greeting was tinged with humor.

She listened to his footsteps retreating down the hallway, a slight pinch of guilt smacking her in the chest for the way she shoved him out of her apartment. Not great day-after behavior, but she'd panicked. She moved into the kitchen area of her apartment, noticing the full coffee pot. Chance must have made it while she was still sleeping.

"Crap." Guilt moved from her chest to settle in her gut. She grabbed her phone from its charger and fire off a text.

Iz: Thanks for making coffee.

After a moment, she rolled her eyes and typed more.

Iz: Sorry for kicking you out. I'm not the greatest with morning afters.

Honestly, she didn't have a lot of them. Whenever she did have a casual hook up, the person usually left before morning. She'd never thought it an issue until Chance pointed out that she deserved better. What did he know? She didn't care if her partner stayed the night. Why would she?

Chance: No problem. And sorry about taking a crack at your fridge. I can be a bit annoying when it comes to nutrition. I took some courses when getting my personal trainer degree. My ex told me I could be a bit too preachy about it. My bad.

She frowned. He hadn't been preachy. A bit overbearing,

sure, but that was just Chance, honestly, he'd been kind of sweet. Which is what freaked her out. They weren't sweet to each other. Fucking Chance was one thing. It was raw and passionate, full of fiery emotions. But sweet...she wasn't sure how to do soft emotions with Chance.

Iz: You're fine. Honestly, I could stand to take my meal prep a little more seriously. I love making baked goods to share with everyone at the studio but cooking full-on meals just for me always feels like a hassle. It's too hard to cook for one.

It always resulted in leftovers and leftovers did not do well in her fridge. She constantly forgot about them until it was too late. Then she had to deal with the mold producing science project in her fridge.

Chance: I could help with that.

Chance: If you want, I mean.

Chance: I know some great recipes that you can portion out and freeze for single meals and easy reheating later.

Of course he did, because Chance knew everything. Only...for once she didn't feel that irritation deep in her chest when he offered unasked for advice. For some weird reason his offer felt less haughty and more...like help. An extending of an olive branch.

Or he wanted back in her bed.

She laughed at the notion. Her body totally for the idea even though her brain knew it was bad. Oh so very bad. Her fingers flew across the screen she sent off a response.

Iz: Are you just angling to get back in my apartment for more sex?

She held her breath, watching those three little dots appear and disappear on the screen. Her stomach pitched, heart pounding furiously, not knowing what answer she wanted him to say.

Chance:...maybe ;)

She laughed, holding her phone tight and shaking her head as a huge smile parted her lips.

Iz: Dream on, O'Brien.

Chance: Don't need to dream, I have a photographic memory and those bad boys will be playing through my head all day.

Iz: Perv. I have work to do, go bother someone else.

Chance: Later Iz.

Iz: Later.

Clutching the phone to her chest, she let out a giggle before tossing the phone on her bed.

"Ugh, he's so annoying."

But the smile was still on her face all throughout the day.

When she arrived at rehearsal that night, a slight pang of disappointment filled her when she saw they were practicing the group routines tonight. She should be relieved she didn't have to work with Chance, but she wasn't. Not wanting to examine that too closely, she chalked it up to the fact that she just wanted to see if their activities last night had gotten rid of her issue with touching him. That was all.

Rehearsal was grueling. The group routine was hard. Much harder than her duo routine with Chance. Timing everything to be in sync with the other four performers in the act was going to be a nightmare, but it would look so amazing once they got it right. Unfortunately for her, Iz was having an issue with the roll down from Lion in the Tree into Alien Neck Hang.

"Hey, Tori."

Her bestie turned as Iz approached her at the end of class.

"Yeah?"

"Can you stay with me for a bit and help me work on that last move. I just can't seem to get it."

Tori smiled. "Yeah sure, babe."

They worked for twenty minutes before Tori got an emergency call from work.

"Shit, I have to go, but I told Meg and Jen I'd lock up the studio after we were done."

"I can do it."

"You sure?"

Iz nodded. Tori breathed out a sigh, relief filling her face. It wasn't a big deal. They'd all learned how to close the studio the first week. Jen and Meg were great about letting people stay late for extra rehearsal. As long as no one ever worked alone. Rule one of aerials.

"Go," she waved her bestie away. "I got this."

Iz moved over to the cleaning bottles, preparing to spray down the mat.

"Thanks, I owe you!"

Tori grabbed her stuff, blowing Iz a kiss on her way out the door.

Iz moved to start cleaning, but the dangling hoop caught her eye. She had come so close to getting the move that last time. If Tori hadn't had to leave, she would have gotten it. She glanced around the silent studio. Everyone had gone home. She was all alone. Her logical brain knew it was a bad idea to even get in the hoop, let alone practice. But she wanted so badly to nail this move. She already felt like a failure because of her poor rehearsal with Chance the other night. If she kept going like this, they'd kick her from the show for sure.

Logic and pride warring within her, Iz placed the spray bottle on the ground and moved to the hoop.

One more time.

Just once more and then she'd go. If she didn't get it this time, she'd pack it up and go.

Grabbing the bottom of the hoop, she straddled up. Once she sat in the hoop she moved until her back rested against the bar, slinging her left leg back and off the hoop she caught it with her right knee adjusting her shoulders until she was comfortably in Lion in the Tree. She placed her hand on either side of her body, cup gripping with her top hand so she could easily grasp the bar and swing under the bar and slid her left shoulder through to get the bar against the back of her neck for the hang.

"Don't think, just do it," she muttered Tori's words to herself. "Use your momentum and don't think too hard. Through the hole, head back and to the side to grip."

Taking a deep breath, she executed the move, shutting her brain off as she felt the motions, allowing her body to take over. She rolled into Alien Neck Hang, feeling the rough grip of the hoop's tape catch the sensitive skin of her neck. She quickly squeezed and gripped the best she could, a surge of pride filling her as she felt her grip secure enough to let go with both hands and hang by only her neck and knee. She'd done it! Finally, she got it!

She started to pull back up into the hoop when the sound of the studio door opening hit her ears. Fear clenched her heart. *Shit!* If anyone caught her practicing alone and told Jen and Meg, she'd be in so much trouble. Oh no! What if it was Jen or Meg? They were the last two people she wanted walking in on her practicing alone.

She moved to dismount from the hoop, but in her haste, her hand missed the grip and she fell to the floor with a thud.

"Iz!"

She breathed a sigh of relief as she recognized the terrified voice calling her name. Thankfully, it wasn't Jen or Meg.

Unfortunately, it was the third least person she wanted to see right now.

"Hey, Chance."

He rushed to her side, kneeling down on the mat and running his hands gently over her body, checking her limbs. "Are you okay? Did you hurt anything when you fell?"

Thankfully, the hoop had been low to the ground, and she was dismounting, so it wasn't really a fall, more of a stumble. Her ass was a little sore, but what part of her wasn't after rehearsal?

"I'm fine."

"What the fuck, Iz?"

She glanced up into his face to see his eyes burning with anger. And something else...fear. He'd been afraid? For her?

"You know you're not supposed to practice alone!" He glared down at her.

She glared right back, sitting up and crossing her arms over her chest. "I wasn't alone. Tori and I were rehearsing, but she got called into work. I was just doing one more thing before locking up."

"*One more thing* is rehearsing alone. You could have seriously hurt yourself and if no one had been here, you could have—"

He sucked in a sharp breath, standing and pacing away from her. She'd never seen Chance this angry. Come to think of it, she'd never really seen Chance angry. Frustrated when he didn't win something, she did, sure. But angry? Never.

"I'm fine."

He turned and the look in his eyes made her breath catch in her throat.

11

The look in his eyes singed her to her very core. Iz sucked in a sharp breath, heat pooling low in her belly. There was fury in Chance's gaze, but behind that, there was something more. Worry, fear...heat.

It was the heat that got to her. Dug deep inside and called to her. She'd promised herself last night would be a onetime thing. Burn off the sexual energy surrounding them and be done with it. But it didn't seem to have worked. Not if the hungry look in his eyes was any sign. Or the throbbing of her body as she stared at him, prowling closer to her as he took distinct, measured steps toward her.

"You could have been hurt," he said, his voice low and rough. "Promise me you won't do it again."

"I don't have to promise you anything," she threw back at him.

Even though she knew he was right, she would never admit it. Practicing alone was a bonehead move, but he didn't get to demand things from her just because they had sex once. Well, one night. It had definitely been more than once. But it wasn't happening again. Nope. Never again.

Chance stopped right in front of her, his hand reaching up to cup the back of her neck. She tried to hide a shiver as her body responded to his touch. The smartass grin on his lips let her know she failed.

"Bet I can make you promise."

She snorted. It was that or haul off and kiss the annoyingly tempting smile right off his face.

"Yeah right."

"Grab the hoop," he commanded.

Iz rolled her eyes, but her damn hands went up of their own volition and grabbed mid-hoop. He eased her back against the apparatus, the bottom of the circle falling right under her shoulder blades. His hands slowly slid down her neck, caressing her skin as he brought them around, stroking her breasts on his path down her body. She sucked in a sharp breath as he maintained eye contact and sunk down to his knees in front of her.

"Chance, what are you..." Her words died when his fingers slid into the waistband of her leggings and tugged them down.

"Convincing you," he said, pulling the pants off her feet one leg at a time and tossing them to the side.

He grasped her thighs, lifting her right leg up and over his shoulder. She felt the soft press of his warm lips against her knee. Her grip tightened on the bar as her body tensed in anticipation. Chance chuckled, trailing a path of gentle, torturous kisses along her inner thigh. Her heart raced, blood pounding in her ears as her core tightened, waiting for his mouth to find it. But as he reached the edge of her panties, the bastard blew a warm breath against her, skipping over all the good bits entirely. He grabbed her left leg, hauling it over his other shoulder and repeated the soft kisses in reverse down to her knee on that side.

"Chance!"

His laughter grated on her nerves. She was seriously going to kill this man. Right after he fucked her. Had to get her orgasm in first.

"Problem, Iz?"

"You know damn well, stop teasing me."

"Not until you promise."

Ugh, this man was infuriating.

"Are you seriously withholding sex until I promise you I'll never practice alone again?"

His hand cupped her ass, massaging in slow, torturous circles while he tugged her so close to his face she could feel the small tickle of his neatly trimmed beard on her inner thighs. She arched her hips, trying to get closer, but it was no use. He wouldn't be swayed until she said the words.

As much as she hated to give Chance anything, he was right. She shouldn't be practicing alone. Her body screamed at her to agree, let him sate the fire he started. While her brain argued her need to be right.

"Izadora," he whispered against her.

So close she could feel the vibration of his words against her clit. That was it. She cracked. Brain be damned. Chance was right, and she was desperate.

"Fine!" She arched her hips against his face. "I won't practice alone ever again, just…please, Chance."

Instantly at her words, his mouth came down against her, hot, wet and open. He kissed her through her cotton panties, soaking the material as his tongue sought her out. She cried out, the sensation glorious, but not enough. He seemed to realize her desperation because one hand left her ass to tug her panties to the side. His tongue thrust inside her. Iz gripped the hoop, sinking down until she was supporting most of her weight on the bottom bar. It dug into her armpits, but she didn't care. All her focus was between her legs on the man doing amazing things to her with his mouth and tongue.

Before long, she found herself screaming his name as the orgasm rushed over her.

"Don't move." She heard Chance say or thought she heard him say. Honestly, the blood was rushing in her ears, she couldn't quite make sense of anything right now.

But then she felt him gently remove her legs from his shoulders, taking her panties down her legs and off as he did. Her wobbly legs somehow sustained her as he moved off to the side, rummaging in his bag for something. She adjusted her grip on the hoop, pulling herself up slightly as she cocked her head, wondering what the hell he was up to.

A huge grin split her lips as she watched him pull a small foil packet from his bag.

"Don't move," he commanded her again.

Normally Chance's commands irritated her, but in this case a small thrill shot up her spine at each strong, sensual, demand. Until she realized what his intent was, then a bit of hesitation crept in. Her grip slipped a bit. "You're not serious."

"I am," he nodded, stripping his pants and boxer briefs off.

His jutting erection momentarily distracted her focus. Her core tightened again, aching for it to fill her. As he ripped open the package and rolled the condom on his length, she shook her head, clearing the fog of lust and asked again, "Chance, you can't seriously be suggesting we have sex in the hoop?"

He stood in front of her, that damn infuriating grin she was coming to crave like water after an intense workout etched on his face. His hands reached down to grasp her thighs. He hooked her legs over his hips, positioning his cock at her entrance.

"Hold on, honey."

She gripped the hoop tighter, the bottom curve pressing into her lower back as Chance thrust inside her.

"Fuck!" she swore, the sensation so good she nearly let her hands fall, but she didn't want to risk them both falling over, so she held tight.

Chance slowly moved in and out. She locked her ankles around his back, arching against the hoop, letting it help hold her weight as he pumped into her. The rough tape of the hoop rubbed against her hands and back, adding such a deliciously opposing sensation to the warm feel of Chance's body against her. He tilted her hips up, so every thrust went deeper. Her grip tightened as something inside her coiled. The intense pressure building, threatening to explode in seconds.

She was torn. It was so amazing she never wanted to stop, but she feared if completion didn't come soon, she just might die.

"Fuck, you feel amazing, Iz," he growled.

"More, Chance. More!" Now it was her turn to command.

He quickened his thrusts, his right hand moving down her hip and to the front so his thumb could rub in her clit in firm round circles. Her hands gripped the hoop so tight she felt the imprint of the tape dig into them. She cried out as her orgasm rushed over her. Chance pumped twice more before following her into oblivion.

Their foreheads pressed together, harsh breath mingling as they came down from their high. She felt the warm strength of his arms wrap around her back as his words whispered in her ear.

"You can let go now. I've got you."

Her heart stilted at those words. She shook off the strange feeling they evoked in her. He only meant she could let go of the hoop, that he had her weight. Nothing more. Silly of her to think any differently. This was just sex. Amazing, absolutely out-of-this-world sex. But still just sex.

Slowly, she pried her hands off the hoop, falling forward and placing her hands around his neck. He moved them a few feet away from the hoop, rubbing her back in soft, comforting circles. Iz nuzzled her face into his neck, inhaling his scent, letting it ground her from the earth-shattering orgasm he'd delivered. Slowly, she removed her legs from his hips, stepping down to the floor. A small whimper escaped her as she felt him slip out of her.

"We should clean up," he said, motioning to the studio bathroom. "You can go first."

She graciously accepted his offer, grabbing up her panties and leggings as she hurried to the bathroom. After she used the facilities and cleaned up the best she could, she tugged her clothing on and motioned for him. While Chance was cleaning up, she grabbed the sanitizing spray and cleaned the hoop and mat, grateful she'd been rehearsing with her own personal hoop tonight. If this thing had been a studio hoop, she'd feel terrible for what they just did in it.

Chance exited the bathroom once she had everything cleaned and put away.

"So..." She shifted on her feet, not sure what to say. What did one say after having logic defying sex with someone they were supposed to dislike?

"Should we keep doing this until it's out of our system?" Chance asked with an arched brow.

She blinked, pondering his words. Why not? Why

shouldn't they keep having sex? Clearly, one night wasn't enough to purge the lust for this man out of her system. They had to keep working together. Why not keep enjoying some benefits while the going was good? As long as they were safe and no expectations were stated, it couldn't hurt, right?

"Yeah." She smiled up at him. "Sounds good to me, but we should probably keep our extracurricular activities to outside the studio."

He tilted his head with a knowing grin. "Why? Didn't like the hoop sex?"

She'd loved it. That was the problem. She'd been so far gone anyone could have walked in and she wouldn't have cared. Jen, Meg, the whole damn cast of the show! Thankfully the studio didn't have any security cameras to catch their little erotic aerial act. Better they keep this thing away from situations that would get them kicked out of the show. And she suspected sex in the studio was a big no-no on that list.

She shrugged. "If that's the only trick you've got in your sexual arsenal..."

He chuckled. "You haven't seen anything yet, honey."

12

"Do I smell cinnamon rolls?"

Chance closed the oven and turned to see Iz sitting up in bed. Sleep still heavy in her eyes, hair adorably disheveled. He took no small amount of pride knowing he'd been the one to give her such wicked sex hair. It had been two weeks since their "let's keep doing this until we're bored" conversation and he'd spent most of those nights in her bed exploring every inch of her body.

"You do."

"But I don't have the stuff to make cinnamon rolls."

She didn't have the stuff to make anything. Iz's food supply was scarily sparse. He knew she worked from home and ordered a lot of delivery or ate out. He could understand that. Cooking for one could be a bit of a chore. But the nutritionist inside him balked at the thought. He might have only taken a class or two of nutrition, but it was enough to know how damaging all that prepackaged and fast-food junk was to the body's systems.

"I ran down to the market on the corner and grabbed some stuff." He poured her a cup of coffee, adding cream and sugar the way he'd learned she liked it. "You said you didn't have work today and I quote 'that means no pants all day' so I figured I better make sure you had some food in the place since most restaurants in the area have a strict pants policy."

Iz snorted. "Yeah right, you probably did it to keep me naked in bed all day and have your wicked way with me."

He winked, handing her the mug. "That too."

She laughed, accepting the coffee and taking a sip with a pleasant sigh. She was right. He enjoyed his time with Iz far more than he ever expected to. The sex was amazing. Off the charts. But it was more than that. He enjoyed being around her. In school, he'd always gotten a thrill from their silly competitions, but now he got a thrill simply by being in her presence. She was smart, beautiful, had a wicked sense of humor, and was a talented and dedicated aerial artist. And while she might not be the most socially graceful person he'd ever met, she tried really hard to be kind and connect with those around her.

Shit! I like her.

Chance took a deep chug of his coffee, hoping his mug obscured any realization on his face. He knew they were sort of friends now and most definitely fuck buddies. They'd come a long way since their nemesis days, but he didn't think Iz would appreciate the knowledge that he'd started to fall for her. She'd either smack him over the head or run screaming.

Both options sounded horrible.

He tucked the information away deep inside to pull out and examine later. No need to ruin the good thing they had going.

"So," he said, sitting on the edge of the bed. "What's on the agenda today?"

Iz picked at some non-existent lint on the blanket, refusing to meet his eyes as she softly said, "Well, um, there's a *Little House on the Prairie* marathon I wanted to catch before it left the streaming services."

"*Little House on the Prairie?*"

She glanced up then, her eyes narrowing on him. "What?"

"Nothing," he chuckled. "I figured you more for a monster movie marathon. Who knew Iz Grant was into bonnets and wagon rides? I think it's kinda sweet."

She rolled her eyes, a small smile playing at the corner of her mouth. Setting down her coffee on the nightstand, she brought her knees up and hugged them to her chest.

"I know, totally not my vibe. But my sister and I used to watch it all the time as kids because it was the only thing on that wasn't news or talk shows."

He knew Iz grew up in a similar situation to him class wise. But unlike his asshole parents, who brought the situation on themselves, making Chance and Cameron suffer for it, Iz's mom was a hard-working single parent doing her best for her daughters. He often wondered what it would have been like to grow up having a parent that cared.

"Anyway," Iz continued, unaware of the dark road his thoughts had turned down. "I saw it was streaming, but I haven't had the time to catch it. I usually do a yearly rewatch with my sister every summer when we get together, but since I'll be touring this summer..."

She'd miss her family time. His chest ached with the loss of his brother. The knowledge that he'd never get family time with Cameron again. He loved that Iz managed to spend time with her sister, but what he wouldn't give for five more minutes with his brother.

Clearing the emotions from his throat, he set his coffee

next to hers and scooted in beside her on the bed, pasting a smile on his face. "Let's go then, John boy."

"That's *The Waltons*," she said with a soft laugh.

"Your knowledge of old televisions shows is very intimidating."

She shoved his shoulder playfully before snuggling into his arms.

Since her studio apartment was so small, they could see her TV from their position snuggled in her bed. Iz clicked on the TV and navigated to the streaming service, clicking on the thumbnail art of the show. He'd never seen more than a few bits and pieces of episodes over the years, and he had to admit the show wasn't really for him, but watching Iz's face as she took in each episode, her mouth moving slightly as she recited the lines she'd memorized over years of rewatches, something deep inside him stirred.

The oven beeped halfway through the first episode. Chance got up to take the cinnamon rolls out. Placing a few on a large plate and bringing it to the bed. The show might not be his thing but spending all day in bed with Iz totally was.

"How many seasons of this show are there?" he asked after their fourth episode.

"Nine."

"Nine?" He hoped she didn't plan on marathoning into the night. It would take weeks to finish the series.

She rolled over into him. With his head propped up against the backboard, the higher angle allowed him to watch the show and her expression. The later he found far more interesting.

Her nose scrunched adorably as she looked up at him with a small wince. "You're hating this, aren't you?"

"No." He wasn't, actually. Couldn't say he cared much for

the show but, "I like that you have something that connects you to your sister. Something special you both share. It's...nice."

"Do you have something like that with your brother?"

Sharp pain cut through him like it always did when he thought of Cameron. There were days he feared the pain would never go away. And other days, he feared it would. He knew it wasn't totally logical, but sometimes he worried if the pain disappeared, his brother would too.

"Cameron's dead." The words were out of his mouth before he could stop them.

"Chance..."

He felt her small hand directly on his bare chest, over his heart. Her touch was warm, but his entire body felt ice cold. It always did when he thought of Cameron. He never talked about his brother. With anyone. So it shocked the hell out of him when he opened his mouth and shared.

"He got sick when I went to college. Leukemia."

"Oh, Chance, I'm so sorry."

She wrapped her arms around his waist and squeezed. He sucked in a sharp breath, allowing himself to take the comfort she offered, even if only for a moment. God, he hadn't realized how desperately he needed it until now.

"My parents were...well you know." It wasn't a secret in their hometown that his parents were the town drunks. They managed enough not to draw the attention of DCFS, but that didn't mean they were any type of functional, caring parental figures.

Iz nodded, her hands softly stroking him, encouraging him to continue.

"Anyway, Cameron got sick my first year of college. I didn't even know until I came home for winter break. He looked so..." His throat threatened to close off. Chance sucked back the emotions and pushed on with his story. "I took him to the doctor because our parents were useless fuckers. He was only 15...he should have been worried about passing his driver's test, not fighting for his life."

Anger boiled up inside him again, anger at his parents, himself, Anger for his brother and a life lost far too soon. Cameron was a good kid. He didn't deserve the fate life handed him. It was so fucking unfair.

"Turns out the cancer had spread too much. There wasn't anything anyone could do. I lost him five months later."

"That's awful."

She pulled him into her, and he went willingly. His head rested on her chest, the steady beat of her heart filling his ears. Iz squeezed him gently, her hands stroking in a soothing manner, and Chance inhaled her scent, taking all the comfort she offered.

"I haven't talked to my parents since the funeral," he confessed. "They should have noticed something. If only they'd taken him to the doctor sooner. If I hadn't gone to school and abandoned him, I could have been there to—"

"No!" She pulled back, cupping his face in her hands and staring down with a hard look. "This is not your fault, Chance. No one can predict when someone will get sick, and you had your own life to start. What happened to your brother wasn't your fault."

He knew that. Logically. His friends at school told him, the therapist he went to see told him, everyone told him. Still, guilt was a hard thing to get rid of. Logic had little power over the bleak, all-consuming emotion.

"I would have noticed sooner if I'd been home."

She lifted a shoulder in a small shrug. "Maybe, or maybe

not. I'm sure you talked to your brother every week when you left, right?"

Memories of late-night phone calls and gif texting wars with his little brother filled his mind, causing a small smile to curl his lips.

"More like every few days."

"See?" She nodded. "You didn't abandon him. You went to college, like tons of young adults do. And you checked in with him regularly. Did he ever mention feeling unwell?"

He let out a harsh breath. "No. Cam never said anything."

Probably because his little brother had known Chance would drop everything and rush back home if he heard Cameron wasn't doing well. Dammit, Cam had been so proud of Chance for getting that scholarship. Of course, he wouldn't have said anything, thinking he would have ruined Chance's opportunities. But the kicker was, Chance would give up every single opportunity in his life if it meant he could have his little brother back.

"Then you can't blame yourself for not knowing. You can't control everything, Chance."

Yeah, but he could try. Because when he didn't look out for the people he cared about...they died.

13

"Y ou need any sticky spray?"

Iz glanced over at Chance who held out a can. They were about to practice their routine. Her mind should have been focused on the moves, but all she could think of was getting the man in front of her out of those tight black leggings he was wearing and finding a few more creative positions they could try in her hoop. Since they were currently surrounded by the entire company, many of whom were casually watching their practice, she figured she should save those thoughts for later.

Holding out her hands she nodded. "Spray me."

Their routine had several spots where she was held aloft by nothing but her grip on Chance or his on her. Sticky spray was a must.

"Okay, music starting," Jen called out as they took their places on either side of the hoop.

Iz stared directly into Chance's eyes as the music played. She silently counted the beats along with him, hand on the hoop, taking measured steps as they slowly spun. At the beat drop they pulled up in unison into side mount, sliding into the hoop, keeping one arm on as they moved into each other, wrapping their free arms around the other's waist, embracing in the hoop.

Whoops and cheers came from their fellow castmates.

"If this impresses them, wait until we get to the flexed foot body hold," Chance chuckled softly against her neck.

"They're just being supportive." Aerialists were the best at hyping each other up. "Now stop distracting me or I'll lose focus and drop your ass on the ground."

"You'd never drop my ass," he said as they came out of the pose and moved into the next. "You like it too much."

Chance winked as she gripped the top of the hoop and hoisting herself up into top of the bar thigh hold.

She grinned down at him. "True fact."

The man did have a delicious backside.

Chance brought his free leg forward and shifted to a straddle back. Once he was in position in star on the bar, legs wide pressing against the hoop, arms out, delightful ass in question on one side as he balanced perfectly upside down, Iz gripped the hoop and slowly flipped. Lowering herself down on top of him. She spread her legs wide against the hoop, back arching as she stared toward the ceiling. The position earned a loud roar of approval from their castmates as well as a few wolf whistles.

Yes, it was a very sensual position. Her crotch was directly on his stomach, ass cradled against his good bits. With any other partner it wouldn't be a big deal, but this was Chance. Half of her brain was focused on the routine while the other half was wondering how they could make this position work without clothes on.

The music played on and while her mind was slightly distracted, she managed to focus on the moves of the routine. Each time they touched—which was a lot—a spark of desire shot through her. She hoped it didn't show on her face, but since this piece was the lovers' duet, she supposed it would be in character to stare at Chance like she wanted to rip off what little clothes he had on and ravage him.

The biggest cheer came at the end as she was finishing her elbow rolls and Chance slid down from inverted handstand on the span set. The piece ended with Chance in top of the bar thigh hold, supporting her with a neck hold while she pushed the hoop away slightly with her foot. It was a beautiful move and required a lot of trust from the baser. As she glanced up into Chance's bright green eyes, she knew there was no one she trusted more to keep her safe.

The thought made her pause slightly, her smile slipping.

"Iz?" Chance's brow furrowed. "You okay? Is my grip not tight enough?"

She shook her head slightly, words caught in her throat. Shaking the errant thought from her mind she brought the hoop back until she could grip it and sit.

"I'm good," she said, finally finding her voice and pulling out of his hold.

He frowned but didn't say anything as she dismounted.

"Great job you two," Jen said, making a note on the notebook in her hand. "Take five."

"I'm gonna grab some water," Iz mumbled, hurrying away from Chance and over to the cubbies where her stuff was.

"You and Chance seem pretty cozy lately."

Iz glanced over at Tori as her friend came up beside her.

"We're just being friendly," she said, shaking off the weird feelings stirring within her. "For the sake of the show."

"Really?" Tori raised a brow.

"Yes, we agreed to be friends, and it worked. He's honestly not that bad anymore."

He wasn't that bad back in high school either, but she had some weird, misguided hard-on for competing with him, which automatically made him her enemy. Iz couldn't help but wonder if she'd spent the time to get to know Chance back then, if they could have been friends...or more.

"Just friends?" her bestie asked with a heavy dose of suspicion.

"Yes, Tori. Just friends."

With benefits, but her bestie didn't need to know that.

"Whatever you say to help you sleep at night, Iz. But that was one of the hottest routines I've ever seen, and I don't just mean the moves. You two were setting that hoop on fire. That man looks at you like you're a snack and he hasn't eaten in a week."

She glanced over to where Chance was warming up across the studio. His gaze was indeed focused on her, raw hunger emanating from his bright green eyes. He sent her a devilish grin that promised her all sorts of wicked things when rehearsal finished. A shiver of anticipation raced down her spine. She heard Tori's soft scoff from beside her as they moved into a lunge position.

"Yeah, just friends, my ass."

Iz ignored her. They were just friends. Did they also enjoy a physical aspect to their friendship? Yes, but that didn't mean anything. Just because she trusted him not to drop her didn't mean she trusted him not to break her heart. He couldn't because she wouldn't give him her heart. She didn't give it to anyone.

"Okay, but be careful," Tori warned. "Banging your duo partner is one thing, but if you all get serious, make sure you're on the same page or someone's going to get hurt. And not in the broken bone falling from the hoop type way."

"It's not...like that," she protested, but her words didn't come out as strong as she'd intended.

Tori searched her face, eyes widening before she sighed softly and shook her head. "Shit, you already fell, didn't you?"

"No!" Her eyes narrowed as she glared. "Can it, Tori, you don't know what you're talking about."

"I'm your best friend, Iz. Who knows you better than me? I know exactly what I'm talking about. A little advice?"

Taking a big sip from her water bottle, Iz waved a hand in the air for her bestie to continue, knowing Tori would whether Iz gave her the okay.

"Talk to him, like really talk, with clothes on."

"Hey!" They talked plenty with clothes on.

"Emotion stuff," Tori said with an insistent gleam in her eyes. "Don't close yourself off like you normally do."

"I don't—"

"You do, Iz," she interrupted. "You hold people at an arm's length, you know you do."

Okay, fine, maybe she did, a little. But being vulnerable with people was hard. It gave them the power to hurt you, leave you. Why risk being crushed under someone's shoes like that? Having your heart ripped into a thousand shreds like what happened to her mom when her dad left? It didn't make sense. How could anyone trust another person like that, knowing it could all end in such misery?

"We're having fun."

Tori raised one eyebrow, disbelief clear on her friend's face.

Whatever. Let everyone believe what they wanted. Iz knew the truth. She and Chance were friends with benefits.

So what if he hung out at her place and cooked her food all the time? He did it so they could stay in bed. Restaurants required pants and she and Chance worked best without them. And just because he watched her comfort show with her—even though she saw him grimace at some episodes— didn't mean he cared. Yes, he'd opened up about his family a little—her heart still ached for him, emotions clogging her throat as she remembered the raw pain still fresh in his eyes as he spoke about his brother—but that didn't mean they were more than what they were.

It didn't mean he cared.

Did it?

Did she?

"Hey, Iz," Jen motioned for her. "Got a second to talk about your duo act? You too, Chance."

A sigh of relief left her. Saved from her internal debate by her director. She allowed her brain to refocus on the task at hand and not on the infuriatingly sexy man who had her all twisted up inside.

"This is looking really great, you two," Jen said when they both made their way to her side. "But I was wondering..."

The show director glanced down at the notebook in her hand. The one she carried around with her filled with notes and the show routines. When she glanced back up, Jen had a spark in her eyes.

"Iz, how comfortable are you with your dislocator?"

Ugh, she hated dislocator. The name alone was horrifying. If you didn't perform it right, you actually could dislocate your shoulders. Iz had gotten the move down a few times, but she hated it. Not that she would tell her boss that. No. Iz plastered a big smile on her face and said, "Love it."

Jen marked something in her notebook. "Excellent. And

how would you feel about going from an elbow roll into dislocator?"

"Wait," Chance held up a hand. "Like as she's spinning? Isn't that kind of dangerous? It takes a lot of flexibility to safely perform a dislocator."

Was he implying she wasn't flexible? Sure she wasn't as flexible as him, but she could do the damn move.

"It is a tricky move." Jen frowned. "I really think it would be dynamite in the act, but I suppose I could put it in another one with more experienced—"

"No!" Iz cleared her throat when Jen's eyes went wide at her loud denial. Giving a soft laugh she smiled. "I can totally do that move. It's not a problem at all."

"You sure?" Jen asked.

"Iz," Chance hissed, leaning in close to whisper to her. "That move is dangerous, I really don't think it's a good idea for you—"

She subtly smashed her foot on his toe, cutting off his quiet protest.

Fury and embarrassment started a low burn in her gut. He was right that the move sounded like a disaster waiting to happen if she couldn't stick it, but that's why they practiced. Besides, this was their boss. Why was he undermining her in front of Jen? Was he trying to make her look bad?

A seed of doubt wiggled its way into her brain. Old habits slinking up to the surface. Their history of always trying to win one over on the other rearing its ugly head. Maybe they hadn't changed as much as she thought. Maybe all this sex had just been that. Sex. All the sharing, the opening up, the sweet gestures...had it all been fake? A ploy to get her to let her guard down so Chance could swoop in and prove he was once again better at everything?

Clenching her fist tight so she didn't haul off and smack him, she faced Jen and smiled.

"I'm game for trying it. I'm sure with practice I can nail it."

"Really?" Jen's worried gaze passed back and forth between Chance, the hoop, and Iz. Doubt crowing into the owner's eyes. "I didn't mean to suggest anything that would make you uncomfortable."

"No, no." She pushed out a small laugh. "I'm happy to learn it. Sounds fun!"

Jen's worried brow eased as she smiled and nodded. "Great. Why don't you come in tomorrow half an hour early and we can work on it together?"

"Perfect."

Jen turned and headed to the front of the studio, calling the end of tonight's rehearsal.

"Iz—"

"Can it, Chance," she said through clenched teeth.

Iz glanced around, but everyone was busy packing up to go home. No one was paying attention to them. Her smile was so tight her cheeks hurt. Turning to face the traitor, she moved closer and spoke in a very hushed and harsh tone. Her words belying the happy appearance fixed on her face. "How dare you."

He blinked, hand going to his chest in shock. "How dare me?"

"Yes, you embarrassed me in front of our boss. Why? To show me up? Prove your better than me? Why, Chance?"

"I was looking out for you," he shook his head with a frown. "That combo is dangerous. I know Jen and Meg want this show to be talked about, but not because one of the performers had to be hospitalized."

"You don't know that would happen. I'm good at what I

do, Chance." The rage was chipping away at her smile. Pretense becoming harder and harder to keep up the more she spoke. "I'm a great aerialist."

"You're phenomenal, Iz. But even a seasoned performer would have trouble with that move."

"I can do it!" she insisted.

"You shouldn't have to," he countered. "The act is great the way it is."

"But it could be better."

She could be better.

Chance stared at her, a sympathetic smile curling his lips as if he knew the thought that popped into her head.

"You're amazing just as you are, Iz. You don't need to keep proving yourself to people."

Iz shifted on her feet, discomfort warring with the rage in her gut. She didn't like that he could so easily read her. When had she let her guard down around this man? And why? Why was it Chance of all people who seemed to see into her soul, know the very things that scared her most?

"Things can always be better," he continued, his voice soft, using that comforting tone he always used in the dark of night after he'd sated her body for the third time. "That's why we keep at them. But it doesn't mean we kill ourselves by overreaching."

"I'm not overreaching. You're overreacting."

His smile slipped, frustration marring the lines on his face as his stare hardened. "I'm trying to protect you."

"I never asked you to!" She never asked for any of this. "You always think you know what's best for everyone Chance, but you don't. You can't control everything and everyone around you. I'm an adult, so strop treating me like a child who doesn't know what's best for herself."

Her breath seized in her lungs, walls closing in. Palms

becoming clammy, sweating through the sticky spray she'd applied earlier. Her heart beat a furious pace in her chest. Everything felt too tight, too loud, too bright. Things had been going so well, but now she felt like she was standing on the precipice, staring down into a dark inky void. One wrong step and she'd fall down, down into the darkness waiting below.

"I know you are, and I know I can be a little...bullheaded at times." Chance stepped forward, grabbing her hands in his. "But it's what you do for the people you love."

Iz's heart stopped. Damn thing skipped a beat, or twenty, before roaring back into overdrive. Panic had her pulling her hands from his. He had not just said that to her in the middle of a fight! What was wrong with him?

"Take it back," she growled.

"What?"

"Take it back. You don't love me."

He quirked a brow. "I don't?"

The panic continued to rise, drowning her as she attempted to swim through the overwhelming sea of emotions she was feeling right now. Shock, joy, fear, hope...

That last one was the killer. Hope was such a bitch of an emotion. It made you dream of things that were out of your control. Working to ace a test, get a job, nail a move. Those things were in her power. But having someone love her and stay with her, for always? How did she control that?

"No. we hate each other."

He laughed. "Pretty sure we don't anymore. In fact, I don't think we ever did."

She'd argue with that, but right now her brain was such a mess of jumbled thoughts and feelings she didn't even know if she could form a coherent sentence. She had to get out of here before she did something stupid, like return Chance's confession.

"Look, this wasn't what I signed up for. We were just having fun."

His arms crossed over his chest, brow furrowing as he stared at her. "Yeah, well, things happen. It's still fun, but now there're feelings involved. So what?"

Feelings. Ugh, what a terrible word. She hated it, she hated this. She'd only recently gotten used to not disliking Chance and now he had to go ruin it by claiming to love her. What kind of psychopath did that?

Fear clawed its way up her throat, but she used ire to push it back down. Ire was good, it was familiar.

"Whatever, it's not your job to protect me, no matter how you feel." She moved to gather up her stuff, digging around in her bag for her keys.

"No matter how *I* feel?" His words sounded behind her, deep and honest. "And how do you feel?"

She sucked in a sharp breath. His question echoing in her head, pulling dreams and wishes from her she never let herself examine before. But then she remembered her mom, the months she spent crying late at night after her dad left, when she thought Iz couldn't hear.

She had.

She thought of all her past relationships. The ones who always told her she was too much, too intense, too closed off, too focused on her goals. No one ever stayed. Not with her. Why would Chance be any different? If she let herself dream, let herself hope, she'd just get hurt again. It was inevitable.

Icy calm washed over her body. She turned and stared him straight in the eye, letting the cold, emotionless state take over as she spoke.

"I feel like getting a good night's sleep so I can come in tomorrow and work on the move Jen knows I can do. I'm sorry, Chance, but we're done."

The shock on his face had her turning and heading to the studio door, but it was the pain in his gaze that made the tears leak from her eyes. She drove home in silence, allowing them to fall as her heart and head fought with each other. All her life she'd been sure of her decisions, but for the first time in her life Iz had no idea if she'd just made the best decision of her life or the worst.

14

A knock on the door interrupted Iz's pity party. It had been two days since her fight with Chance. Two days since she started rehearsing the new move with Jen. They'd practiced and practiced, and she had managed to get the move down. Jen had been ecstatic. Chance had stoically offered his congratulations. But the win didn't feel as good as it should have.

Normally Iz would be gloating over proving herself right. Basking in the glow of her accomplishment. So why did she feel so...empty? Something was wrong, and she didn't want to put her finger on it because she feared she knew exactly why her win didn't feel like a win.

"Izadora, I swear if you don't open this door up right now!"

She sighed at the sound of her bestie's growl, muffled from beyond her closed apartment door. Rising off her bed, she trudged over to the door and opened it.

"Hey, Tori." she greeted her friend.

"Don't you 'hey Tori' me." Tori pushed her way inside.

"By all means, come in." Iz deadpanned as she closed her door.

Tori glanced around, turning with a raised brow. She knew what her friend saw. Messy bed with unwashed sheets because she couldn't bring herself to erase Chance's scent from them. Dishes piled high in the sink because she'd lost the motivation to clean. Fast food wrappers everywhere because Iz didn't cook for one and the one person who had treated her to his mouthwatering meals was gone.

Because I pushed him away.

"This place looks worse than the time Winnie broke up with you." Tori nudged at a dirty sock on the floor with her foot.

"She didn't break up with me. I broke up with her," Iz insisted.

"Only because she gave you an ultimatum, move in together or break up and you panicked and picked the latter."

True. But Winnie hadn't been right for Iz. Her ex-girlfriend never really supported her aerial dreams. She thought it was a silly hobby, not a passion literally burning in Iz's soul. They never would have made it through a year with Iz on tour.

"What happened with Chance, Iz?"

She lifted her chin, shoulders going rigid as the past few days flew through her mind. Iz opened her mouth fully prepared to tell her best friend that nothing happened. Everything was fine. But to her absolute horror, when she started to speak, nothing but a mournful sob came out.

"Oh, sweetie," Tori opened her arms.

Iz rushed into her friend's embrace. They stood in the middle of her chaotic, depressed mess of an apartment as Tori let Iz get it all out. Once the tears slowed down, her friend moved them to the couch. Tori passed over a box of tissues and sat quietly as Iz explained everything. Starting with her and Chance's agreement to be fake friends, how they tried to burn off their attraction to each other, and their fight the other night, ending everything.

"So," Tori said slowly, tilting her head as she took in everything Iz said. "Let me get this right. You two faked a friendship that turned into fucking, which lead to a real friendship and even feelings, and now you're throwing it all away because he doubted you could do a move?"

"No." Iz realized the past few days that she had been using that as an excuse. A convenient refrain from her past. An easy out so she could ignore all the messy, complicated emotions running through her. Emotions she had no idea what to do with. All her bluster about Chance sabotaging her, trying to make her look bad in front of Jen, it was all a front to cover up the real reason she threw up walls against him.

"He said he loves me." The confession flew from her lips on a quiet whisper.

Tori sat silently for a full minute before she blinked, a smile curling her lips. "Oh, I see now."

"What?"

"You panicked." Her friend patted her hand. "Izadora Grant, you are my best friend and I love you to pieces but you, babe, have a serious problem with connecting."

She scowled. "I do not!"

"You do." Tori nodded. "Always have. You don't like people seeing you as vulnerable."

Who did? Exposing your weakness to people was a sure way to allow them to use it against you. What was wrong with putting up a strong front all the time?

"It's okay to let your guard down around people who

care about you, Iz. And if Chance said he loves you, then he does."

"But..." Her hands trembled, doubt making her voice small as she voiced her fear. "But how do I know he really loves me? How do I know it's real?"

Tori shrugged. "You just have to trust. Trust him, trust your feelings."

Right, like it was that easy.

"I know you guys had your issues in high school, but watching you two together these past weeks, I'm only talking from my perspective, but it looks like you two really click. He looks at you like he cares, Iz. And I know he's spent a lot of time over here with you."

"He cooked for me," she confessed, a sad smile turning her frown up. "And he watched *Little House on the Prairie* with me."

Tori's eyes went wide. "Holy hell, the man does love you."

Iz laughed. Her best friend refused to watch that show with her, claiming it was less exciting than watching paint dry.

"Seriously, Iz. Look really deep inside and admit you're scared."

She would do no such thing. Izadora Grant wasn't scared of anything!

But just because she was curious, she glanced over at her bestie, voice trembling as she asked, "Scared of what?"

"Scared that you might love him too."

The words smacked into her brain, ringing in her ears, loud clanging bells of truth forcing her to wake up and listen. She moved back over the events of the past month. The past years. Her entire relationship with Chance. They'd always competed, but she had to admit there was never any animosity to it. Chance always played fair, and truth be told, he celebrated her wins as much as his own. Yes, he was obnoxiously bossy, but she now understood that simply came from a place of caring. He wanted to look out for those he loved. And it seemed he loved...her.

A small squeak of joy left her lips as it finally sunk in.

He loved her.

And she loved him. There was no denying it anymore. She loved competing with him, rehearsing with him, arguing, and laughing with him. She loved spending all day in bed with him, watching TV or seeing who could give who the most orgasms. She loved just being near him.

"I love Chance." She glanced over at Tori, her head shaking in disbelief. "I fucking love Chance O'Brien. How did...what...?"

Tori rolled her lips in, suppressing laughter. "Yes, sweetie. You do and since he said he loved you too, I suggest you get off your self-pitying ass and go tell the man you're sorry and that you love him. But after you take a shower, because you smell like hamburgers and misery."

A happy sob of laughter escaped her. She couldn't believe she almost wrecked everything because she'd been too mired in her own fears to see the truth. Now all she had to do was hope there was still time to set things right.

CHANCE STOOD at his brother's gravestone, staring at the name carved into it. The dates below. The saying inscribed on the cold gray slate:

Cameron Austin O'Brien
Beloved brother and son.
Gone too soon,

but always in our hearts.

"I'm doing it, Cam," he whispered into the small stirring of wind, touching the chain around his neck with his medallion engraved with his brother's name on it. "I head off on a worldwide tour next week and you're coming with me. We'll see the world, like we always planned."

He was keeping his promise to his brother. He couldn't save him, but he could make sure Cam was always with him. Always remembered. The moment was bittersweet as he stood there. Happiness at seeing his brother's last wish come true, muted by the pain of loss. Multiple losses.

He shouldn't have questioned Iz's abilities the other night. He knew she was a skilled aerialist. She was damn good. But when Jen had proposed such a dangerous trick... he'd panicked. All he could think of was Iz getting hurt. He knew how much she pushed herself. She'd never say no, never give up, even if it meant...

His heart had frozen, fear clawing its way up his throat as his worst nightmare flashed before his eyes. The thought of losing another person he loved had been too much to take. So, he'd brashly spoken out. Gone all bossy as she claimed and made her look bad in front of their boss. Even if it wasn't his intention, it still came across that way, and he was so damn sorry.

Watching Iz perfect the move these past two days had been terrifying. Every slip and miss, he'd wanted to run in and save her. But she didn't need him to save her. She'd been right. He couldn't save the people he loved. No matter how hard he tried. He hadn't been able to save Cameron. No one had, not the doctors, not the medicine. It fucking sucked, but it was what it was.

"I need to learn to let it go, Cam," he spoke to his brother's grave, moisture gathering in his eyes. "I am so sorry I couldn't help you and I'm going to try really hard not to be so...overprotective of the people in my life anymore. Thanks for being the best little brother a guy could ask for."

Bending down, he placed a hand on the cold, hard granite, letting the guilt flow out of him. He'd always hold a bit with him, he knew that, but it was time to stop blaming himself for something completely out of his control.

He turned and started to head out of the cemetery when a figure a few feet away stopped him right in his tracks. His jaw dropped as he stared at the vision before him.

"Iz?" He blinked, but she didn't disappear. "What are you doing here?"

She stood before him in a pale blue sundress that complimented her peach-colored hair, which hung in loose waves around her shoulders. A hesitant smile curled her lips as she moved toward him.

"Your, um, roommate Darnell said you'd be here. I didn't want to interrupt..."

"You're not. I was just..." He glanced back at his brother's grave. "Cam always wanted to travel the world. We planned on doing it when he got out of high school, but then...I was just coming to tell him we're doing it."

Glancing back at her, he clutched his necklace. "One of the reasons I wanted to go on this tour was to fulfill that promise to my brother."

"Oh, Chance." Her eyes filled, but she blinked, and the moisture disappeared. "That's wonderful. I know he'll be with you in your heart every step of the way."

He nodded. "Was there something you wanted?"

"Yes." She took a deep breath and stepped closer. "I wanted to apologize for what I said the other night at rehearsal. I know I can be a bit...defensive when people question my abilities. I realize now you weren't being malicious or trying to sabotage me. You were looking out for me."

"I was scared," he confessed. "But that was no excuse for me doubting you in front of Jen."

He reached out and grasped her hands in his. "You're an amazing aerialist, Iz. I know that and I have no doubts you can perfect any move given to you. I'm sorry if I made it seem like I was—"

"Hey," she laughed, tugging on his hands and pulling him closer. "This is my apology. Stop trying to do it better than me."

He grinned. "Oh, so you're the best at apologies?"

"Yes," she tilted her chin up. "And I'm also the best at groveling, so please, Chance O'Brien, accept my apology for acting like a scaredy-cat and lashing out at you instead of admitting the truth."

His heart pounded as her words caused a flame of hope to rise within him. "The truth?"

Her gaze locked on his, emotions pouring out from their brown depths. Her hands trembled in his as her lips parted, a small breath escaping before she confessed.

"I love you, Chance."

Weight fell from his shoulders. Fear and doubt blasted away by pure, unfettered joy. He'd been aching to hear those words from her ever since his confession. Terrified that the day would never come. That he was wrong. She didn't care for him the way he cared for her.

"Okay." He nodded. "You win. You're the best at apologies."

She smiled, bright and happy and so damn beautiful he couldn't stop himself from swooping down and covering her lips with his own. She opened for him, throwing her arms around his neck and pressing close while he tasted the heaven that was Izadora Grant. He could feel every ounce of her love in the kiss, every fear banished, every hope burning bright. When she pulled away, he chuckled at the absurdity of what they'd just done. Started a new beginning in a place built for endings.

A small beeping sound filled the air and Iz's eyes went wide.

"Oh shit! Chance, we're going to be late for rehearsal."

She tugged on his hand, pulling him away from his past and into the future.

"IF YOU ROLL YOUR CLOTHES, you'll have more space in your suitcase."

Iz glanced up from her packing, arching one brow in Chance's direction at the end of her bed. He held up his hands with a wince.

"Sorry, not trying to tell you how to pack. Simply offering a suggestion."

She laughed softly, tossing down the pajama pants she was folding and moving over to place a soft kiss to his lips. "I appreciate the suggestion and I'll take it under advisement."

The past few days since their talk at the cemetery had been a whirlwind. Dress rehearsals had started, and they were leaving on their tour in two days. Chance had stayed over at her place every night. They'd talked, laughed, made love. He'd only returned to Darnell's place to grab his stuff and drop off the snickerdoodle cookies she made, since Chance's friend said they were his favorite.

As she rolled her clothes and started putting them in her suitcase, finding that it did indeed provide more space, she grumbled without any heat, "You're right."

"I'm sorry?" Chance's voice lit with humor. "What was that again? I couldn't hear you."

Failing to hide her smile, she crossed her arms over her chest and stuck her tongue out at him. "You were right about the packing, but you have to admit I was right about the burger place we tried last night."

Chance grinned, grabbing her around the waist and pulling her into him. "I'll never doubt your culinary suggestions again."

She snorted, a small sigh escaping her as he nibbled on that sweet spot on her neck right below her ear.

"Chance." A soft moan left her lips as her eyelids drifted closed. "We still have packing to do."

"Pack later," he murmured in her ear. "Need you now."

The man did have good ideas and Iz had given up trying to fight them. Especially when they benefited her too. She turned, gently placing her suitcase on the floor before tugging Chance onto the bed with her.

"I love you," he said, bright green eyes staring into hers.

She'd never get tired of hearing those words. Never get used to the joy they filled her with. Cupping his cheek, she smiled as the rough bristles of his trimmed beard tickled her hand. "I love you too," she whispered back.

She never imagined she'd find someone she felt safe enough with to let her walls down. Someone she could expose her vulnerabilities to. Someone she could be one hundred percent herself with and still have them love her. But she had found that, with him. If anyone had told her even a year ago that her high school nemesis would turn out to be the love of her life she would have laughed in their face, but here she was.

"So, what are we competing for this time? Orgasms? Most creative position?" he asked, bobbing his eyebrows.

She shook her head. "Nothing, because I've already won your heart."

He was stock still for a moment before he burst into laughter, his head falling to her chest as the rumbles of his chuckles vibrated against her skin. When he lifted his head, he smiled at her.

"That was super cheesy."

"Hey!" She playfully swatted his shoulder. "I was going for romantic."

"Very romantic, babe." He kissed the tip of her nose, brushing his lips against hers as he whispered, "And I won your heart too."

"Damn right you did."

And she'd never been so happy to lose anything in her entire life.

The End

ABOUT THE AUTHOR

Bestselling author Mariah Ankenman lives in the beautiful Rocky Mountains with her two rambunctious children and loving spouse who is her own personal spell checker when her dyslexia gets the best of her.

Mariah loves to lose herself in a world of words. Her favorite thing about writing is when she can make someone's day a little brighter with one of her books. To learn more about Mariah and her books visit her web site:

https://mariahankenman.com/

follow her on social media or sign up for her newsletter.

ALSO BY MARIAH